Mom, There's a Pig in My Bed!

FRANCESS LANTZ has written eighteen books for children and young adults. She lives with her husband and her dog, Amigo, in Santa Barbara, California, in a house overlooking a canyon full of chapparal, gophers, scrub jays, and hawks. When she isn't writing she enjoys bodyboarding, playing the drums, and pigging out on Texas barbeque.

During her childhood she had lots of pets—two dogs, a cat, turtles, frogs, fish, and a four foot long snake, but—alas—no pigs.

Mom, There's a Pig in My Bed!

FRANCESS LANTZ

AN AVON CAMELOT BOOK

MOM, THERE'S A PIG IN MY BED! is an original publication of Avon Books. This work has never before appeared in book form. This work is a novel. Any similarity to actual persons or events is purely coincidental.

AVON BOOKS
A division of
The Hearst Corporation
1350 Avenue of the Americas
New York, New York 10019

Copyright © 1992 by Francess Lantz
Published by arrangement with the author
Library of Congress Catalog Card Number: 91-93039
ISBN: 0-380-76112-2
RL: 4.7

First Avon Camelot Printing: April 1992

CAMELOT TRADEMARK REG. U.S. PAT. OFF. AND IN OTHER COUNTRIES, MARCA REGISTRADA. HECHO EN U.S.A.

Printed in the U.S.A.

OPM 10 9 8 7 6 5 4 3 2

For Jane Anstine Benge,
my wonderful fifth-grade teacher,
who read my crazy stories and cheered instead of laughed.

And with thanks to
Cia Hosea, Mary Ann Evans, Brian Burd, Steve Keltz,
and Hamlet the pig.

Chapter One

Jody Ewing was hiding under her bed, pretending to be a dangerous bank robber. She was just about to grab the money and make a run for it when she heard her mother yell, "Dwight! Jody! Jeremy! Time to make the Mishmash!"

Mishmash Surprise was the Ewing family's usual Friday-night dinner. It was also Jody's favorite meal in the whole world. In fact, there was only one thing she liked better than eating Mishmash Surprise, and that was making it.

Jody leaped up and ran full-speed into the kitchen. Her curly red hair flew back from her face and her blue eyes sparkled. She crouched down behind the kitchen table and pointed an imaginary gun at an imaginary policeman. "You'll never take me alive, copper!" she cried. "Pow! Pow! Urgh, they got me!" She grabbed her heart, groaned dramatically, and fell dead on the floor.

Mrs. Ewing just smiled. "Why don't you be the police officer once in a while?" she asked.

Jody came back to life and sat up. "Because the bad guys get all the good death scenes."

She hopped to her feet as her big brother Dwight came into the room. He had freckles and neatly combed brown hair, and he was wearing his usual outfit—gray slacks and a button-down, pin-striped shirt. "I just counted the money in my piggy bank," he announced. "I have almost fifty dollars in there."

"You mean you cracked open your bank?" Jody asked in disbelief. "The one Grandpa Ewing gave you when you were born?"

"I only knocked out a little hole under the left rear hoof. It looks almost as good as new."

"But Dwight," Mrs. Ewing said, "that's supposed to be part of your college fund."

"Piggy banks are for little kids," he said with disdain. "In a real savings bank that money would be earning interest. Or even better, I could invest it in the stock market—"

"Hey, look what I found!"

Everyone turned to see Jeremy, the youngest Ewing, standing in the doorway. In his outstretched hands he held a fat black garden slug.

"You're not keeping that thing in our bedroom," Dwight said immediately.

"She's not a thing. She's my new pet, and her name is Rosie." Jeremy pushed his glasses up his nose and smiled. "Because I found her under the rose bushes."

"Jeremy, why do you have to collect such disgusting pets?" Jody asked. "Next thing we know, you'll be bringing home a black widow spider."

"Well, if I could just have a dog . . ."

"Jeremy," Mrs. Ewing interrupted, "you know perfectly well your father is allergic to dogs. And cats. And—"

"—any animal with a lot of hair," Jeremy intoned. "I know, I know."

"Here," Mrs. Ewing said, reaching under the sink for an empty mason jar. "Rosie can live in this until we find something better. We'll poke a few holes in the top so she can breathe."

After the slug had been installed in its new home, Mrs. Ewing opened the refrigerator and took out all the leftovers from the past week. "Okay," she said, "let's see what we've got."

Jody peeled the plastic wrap from the first storage bowl. "Two slices of meat loaf," she announced.

Jeremy opened the second. "Macaroni and cheese! My favorite!"

Jody made a face. "I found some lima beans, only they look kind of furry."

"Throw them out," Mrs. Ewing instructed.

"Hey, I've got an idea," Dwight broke in. "Why don't we throw out all the leftovers and go to McDonald's for a change?"

Jody stared at her brother in disbelief. "Anyone can go to McDonald's. Eating Mishmash Surprise is special."

"Specially weird, you mean."

Jody frowned. *It's not the Mishmash Surprise that's weird,* she thought, *it's you.*

Ever since Dwight had entered junior high, he'd been acting peculiar. Take his clothes, for example. He used to love the outfits that Mrs. Ewing designed and sewed for the family. Nowadays though, he refused to wear anything that didn't have a designer label on it. Or take money, for another thing. Lately, it was all he talked

3

about. He even read the *Wall Street Journal*! It was just plain weird.

Mrs. Ewing placed the big stew pot on the stove. "Okay, kids," she said, "start dumping."

Jody put Dwight out of her mind and turned her attention back to the Mishmash. With Jeremy's help, she tossed all the leftovers into the pot. Aside from the meat loaf and the macaroni and cheese, there was a cup of peas, some chicken, five pieces of fried tofu, some mushroom soup, and a baked potato.

Mrs. Ewing added one cup of beef stock and some spices. Then she put on the lid and turned up the heat. "Mishmash Surprise, coming right up." She took five plates out of the cupboard. "Better set the table. Your father will be home any minute."

Jody carried the plates, Dwight carried the glasses, and Jeremy carried the napkins. There was no silverware, because on Mishmash Night the Ewings ate with their hands.

"You know, I bet Dad could sell his idea for Mishmash Surprise and make a lot of money," Dwight said as he put down the glasses.

"But Mishmash Surprise is leftovers," Jody said. "How do you convince people to buy leftovers?"

"You don't. What you sell is the concept." He held one of the glasses in front of his mouth like a microphone and said, "Ladies, don't throw away those old leftovers! Turn them into a delicious dinner with Ewing's Leftovers Helper. Just put all your leftovers into a large pot and toss in one package of Ewing's delicious blend of herbs, spices, and flavor enhancers. Turn on the heat, and that's it. In less than thirty minutes you'll have a dinner the whole family will love."

He thrust his imaginary microphone into Jody's face

and said, "Just listen to the words of this typical American housewife."

"It's true," Jody exclaimed in a cheery voice. "Ewing's Leftovers Helper makes anything taste good. Why, once I threw an old sweat sock into the pot by mistake and my family ate it right up!"

Jeremy pulled off his sock and pretended to gobble it down. "Oh, Mommy," he cried, "this is so yummy!"

Dwight and Jody burst out laughing. Jeremy giggled and took a few more imaginary bites.

But suddenly Dwight wasn't laughing anymore. "Dad's always inventing stuff," he said, "but he never makes any money off his inventions. And you know why?" He didn't wait for an answer. "Because he doesn't know how to promote them."

Jody thought it over. Her father was a great inventor, there was no doubt about that. Last year he invented a house paint that changed color when it got wet. For Christmas he built Dwight an "alarm mattress"—a mattress that tossed him out of bed when it was time to get up. And, of course, he invented Mishmash Surprise.

But Mr. Ewing only invented things for fun. He never thought about making money from his inventions. Neither did anyone else in the family—until now.

Jody's thoughts were cut short when she heard her father's key in the lock. "Daddy's home!" she cried. She ran into the living room and threw herself into her father's arms. Dwight and Jeremy were right behind her.

As usual, Mr. Ewing's glasses had slipped halfway down his nose and the breeze had blown his shaggy hair across his forehead. But what was *not* usual was the look on his face. Normally, Mr. Ewing was all smiles when he came home from work. But tonight he looked distracted—or maybe even worried.

"How was your day, Daddy?" Jody asked.

Mr. Ewing frowned. "Oh . . . all right, I guess. All right. How about you?"

Dwight, Jody, and Jeremy began talking at the same time. It came out something like this: "In school today I . . . selling Mishmash Surprise . . . a part in the sixth-grade play . . . to make some money . . . and found a slug."

"That's nice," Mr. Ewing said vaguely. "What's for dinner?"

"Don't tease, Daddy." Jeremy giggled. "You know we eat Mishmash Surprise every Friday night."

"Oh, yes. Yes, of course."

Just then, Mrs. Ewing walked into the dining room with the stew pot. Eagerly, the children ran to the table. It wasn't an ordinary square table, or a rectangular one, or even a round one. The Ewings' table was curved on two sides and zigzagged on the other two. The top of it was covered with bumps and valleys like a big relief map of the world. Mr. and Mrs. Ewing had built the table with Jeremy, to teach him how to use tools.

When the whole family was seated, Mrs. Ewing served the Mishmash. Everyone grabbed hunks of homemade bread to mop up the sauce. Then they all rolled up their sleeves and dug in with their hands.

The Mishmash was so good that nobody noticed how quiet Mr. Ewing was being. But when Jody finished eating, she saw that he hadn't cleaned his plate. That was so unusual, she felt a little worried. "Daddy," she asked hesitantly, "are you feeling okay?"

"Yes," he said. "Well, that is to say . . . I have something to tell all of you."

6

"What is it?" Mrs. Ewing asked.

"Let's have dessert," he replied. "I always like to eat something sweet while I'm saying something sour."

Jeremy ran into the kitchen and brought back the Mishmash Pudding. This week's Mishmash included vanilla custard, strawberry yogurt, a half a glass of chocolate milk, and two oatmeal cookies—all mixed together in the blender and topped with whipped cream.

Mr. Ewing took a big bite of Mishmash. Then he looked at his family and said, "It's about my job . . ."

Mr. Ewing had worked at the Ideal Box Company for almost six months. His job was to design new kinds of boxes. His boss, Mr. Mobley, would explain what they wanted to put in the boxes—computers, or screws, or maybe farm equipment—and then Mr. Ewing would design them.

"Did you get a raise?" Dwight asked hopefully.

"I'm afraid not." Mr. Ewing put down his spoon. "I was fired," he said sadly.

This wasn't the first time Mr. Ewing had been fired. In fact, for as long as Jody could remember her father had been going from one job to another. The problem was his inventions. He worked on them when he was supposed to be doing his regular job, and that got him in trouble.

"What happened this time?" Mrs. Ewing asked.

"I was supposed to be designing boxes to put frozen swordfish in," Mr. Ewing explained. "But then I had the most interesting idea. Why not make a carpet out of living grass? Can't you just see it? Wall-to-wall grass carpeting!"

Whenever Mr. Ewing talked about his inventions, his face changed. His eyes took on a special faraway look, as if he were seeing something magical floating in the middle of the sky. His eyebrows lifted, and three deep wrinkles formed across his forehead. Then his voice dropped to a husky whisper and his words sounded like poetry.

"Imagine coming home from a hard day at work or school, slipping off your shoes, and stepping on soft, cool grass. So much more welcoming than synthetic carpeting. And imagine the smell—like softball games, and picnics, and starting up the lawn mower on a warm summer morning."

Dwight's voice broke the spell. "But what *happened*, Dad?" he insisted. "Why did they fire you?"

Mr. Ewing blinked his eyes like a sleeper awakening from a beautiful dream. "Mr. Mobley discovered me out by the parking lot, collecting grass samples for my prototype carpet," he said. "I tried to explain about wall-to-wall grass carpeting, but he told me I was a kook. Then he fired me."

Jody felt like crying. Her father wasn't a kook; he was a genius. Why couldn't other people understand that? It just wasn't fair.

Mr. and Mrs. Ewing had started talking about unemployment benefits and car payments and a lot of other things Jody didn't understand. To make herself feel better, she took a big bite of Mishmash Pudding. But tonight the pudding stuck to the roof of her mouth like sickeningly sweet rubber cement, and she had to force herself to gag it down.

With an unhappy sigh, Jody pushed away her bowl. When her father was out of work, nothing seemed right—not even Mishmash Pudding.

8

Chapter Two

It was Saturday afternoon, a week later, and Jody and Jeremy were in the backyard, playing kick the can with a group of kids from the neighborhood. Dwight sat on the back steps, glancing through one of Jody's Spiderman comic books and watching them. He'd much rather have been hanging out at the mall with his friends, but until his parents came back from the supermarket, he was stuck there, keeping an eye on his younger brother and sister.

"Come play with us, Dwight," Jeremy called.

"Naw, I'm busy."

"Oh, come on," Jody urged. "You don't even like Spiderman. Besides, Jeremy is 'it.' "

"You better watch out," Jeremy teased. "If you're still here after I kick the can, I'm going to tag you."

Dwight hated to disappoint his brother. "Oh, all right," he said, tossing aside the comic. "Just for a little while."

"Hurray!" Jeremy shouted. He kicked the battered

9

soup can and the kids took off, scattering in every direction like mice let out of a cage.

Dwight ran around the house and hid in the azalea bushes beside the garage. He was crouching there, trying not to get dirt on his new pants, when he heard his mother's voice coming from inside the garage.

"Every night you circle job listings in the paper," Mrs. Ewing was saying. "But the next day, instead of calling to set up interviews, you come in here and lock the door."

Dwight knew he wasn't supposed to eavesdrop, but he was curious. Besides, he couldn't leave the bushes now or he'd be tagged. He pressed his ear against the side of the garage and waited to hear more.

"I'm creating the world's first grass carpet," Mr. Ewing said proudly. There was a pause, and then he spoke in a much different voice. "I don't know. Maybe I'm crazy. Who'd want to buy a grass carpet, anyway?"

Good question, Dwight thought. But his mother had an answer.

"I'd buy it," she said. "I'd buy anything you invented. You're the only person I ever met who sees the world as a big toy just waiting to be played with. That's a gift, you know."

"But there's no money in it."

"Listen," Mrs. Ewing said suddenly, "maybe *I* should look for a job."

"But you already have a job," Mr. Ewing protested.

Mrs. Ewing designed and made clothing—unique, unusual clothing, like shirts decorated with bottle tops and rain hats made out of autumn leaves. She sold her clothes at a local boutique called Fashionably Yours. Not many people bought them, but the owners liked to

10

display them in the window because they brought people into the store.

"Forget it," Mr. Ewing said. "If you stop designing clothes and get a regular job, you'll be just as unhappy as I am." He paused. "There's got to be a solution to our problem. Some way to make money doing what we love. Not a lot of money—just enough to get by."

"I wish I knew how," Mrs. Ewing said.

Dwight leaned against the side of the house and rested his chin on his knees. Why did he have to have such goofy parents? All his friends had mothers and fathers with normal jobs—doctors, insurance salesmen, stock-brokers, things like that. They didn't spend their time inventing crazy-colored house paint or knitting hats out of multicolored telephone wire.

Dwight flicked an ant off his sleeve. It wouldn't be so bad, he decided, if only his parents had the slightest bit of business sense. But making money didn't come naturally to them, the way it did to Dwight. To him, ideas like selling the Mishmash Surprise concept to a big food company were as obvious as the nose on his face. But if he suggested it to his father, he knew what the answer would be. "Oh, I don't know how to talk to those corporate types," Mr. Ewing would say. "Besides, Mishmash is just for fun."

Dwight sighed. *If this family is ever going to make any real money,* he told himself, *it's going to be up to me to do it.* He thought about the fifty dollars he had liberated from his piggy bank. *If only Mom and Dad would let me invest it,* he thought, *I just know I could make a profit.*

He closed his eyes and pictured himself sitting behind a big desk, buying and selling stocks and bonds and commodities. "Sell AT&T," he imagined himself

11

shouting into the phone, "and buy a million dollars' worth of IBM. No, make that two million!" He smiled dreamily. Now *that* was the way to make a killing!

"Gotcha!" Jeremy lunged into the bushes and tagged Dwight hard on the shoulder. The tag brought him back to earth with a bump. He wasn't a wealthy investor, buying and selling millions of dollars worth of stocks. He was just an unhappy kid with an off-the-wall family and a father who was out of work.

"Okay, okay, you got me," Dwight said irritably. With a frown, he trudged into the backyard to join the others who had already been tagged.

The next day was Lefty day. All the Ewings were right-handed, but once a week they did everything with their left hands, just for fun.

"Maybe I should start my own business," Mr. Ewing suggested at breakfast. He carefully spooned his cereal with his left hand. "I could turn the garage into a store and sell my inventions."

"I thought of that," Mrs. Ewing said. "But Shirley at Fashionably Yours told me most businesses lose money the first two years. We don't have enough savings to see us through."

"You would if you invested it," Dwight broke in. "I've been reading about the stock market and the commodities market—"

"Since when have you been interested in the commodities market?" Mr. Ewing asked incredulously.

"Since we did a unit on economics in social studies. I thought about how we're so broke all the time," Dwight said, "and I realized we don't have to be. For example, if we invested in pork bellies—"

"Pork bellies?" Jody gasped. "You mean like pig guts?"

Dwight gave her a withering look. "No, dummy. It means the part they make bacon out of." He turned to his father. "I've got almost fifty dollars in my piggy bank. Now, if I invested that in pork bellies, at today's rate—"

"If I can't have a dog or a cat," Jeremy interrupted, "how about a pig?"

"Jeremy," Dwight said in exasperation, "we are not talking about pigs." He grabbed his butter knife with his right hand.

"Right is *wrong!*" Jeremy shouted, pointing at Dwight's hand. "You forgot to use your left hand!"

Dwight groaned and switched hands. The first person to use his right hand on Lefty Day had to wash all the dinner dishes, and Dwight hated washing dishes.

Jody used her spoon to make a tidal wave in her cereal. "Cereal is boring," she said. "Can I make myself a bacon and tomato sandwich?"

Mrs. Ewing laughed. "I detect a definite pig theme to this morning's breakfast."

"Pigs are smart," Jeremy said. "Like Wilbur in *Charlotte's Web.*"

"Wilbur was a make-believe pig," Jody said. "Besides, he wasn't so smart. It was Charlotte who had all the brains."

"But, in fact, pigs *are* highly intelligent," Mr. Ewing said. "More intelligent than dogs, they say. I read an article about it in the *Smithsonian* once."

"That's great," Dwight said impatiently. "But what do you say, Dad? Can I invest my fifty dollars in pork bellies? Please? It's a sure thing, practically. Why, if I don't make money, I'll . . . I'll kiss a pig!"

13

Jeremy giggled. "Oink, oink!" he grunted. "Give me a kiss, Dwight. I'm Wilbur!" Then he pointed to the glass of orange juice in Dwight's right hand. "Right is *wrong*!"

"Oh, no!" Dwight moaned. "You caught me again."

"See?" Jeremy said with a grin. "I told you Wilbur was smart!"

That afternoon, Jody was in Jeremy's room, reading him a picture book called *Missy: Seeing-Eye Dog*. It was all about a German shepherd named Missy who was trained to be a seeing-eye dog. At the end of the book, she went to live with a blind woman named Suzanne.

"If I was blind like Suzanne," Jeremy said wistfully, "Mom and Dad would *have* to let me get a dog."

"Don't be silly," Jody replied. "Being blind would be awful, with or without a dog."

"I know, but it's fun to pretend. Watch!" He closed his eyes and walked slowly across the room. "See, Jody, I'm blind."

"Hey, let me try," Jody said, jumping up to join him.

With his eyes still closed, Jeremy turned to face her. "I've got a better idea. You can be my seeing-eye dog. Get down on all fours."

Jody laughed. "Okay," she agreed, dropping to her knees. "Woof," she barked to let him know she was ready.

Jeremy held her shirttail and Jody the Seeing-Eye Dog led him down the hall. "Take me to Daddy's workshop," he instructed.

Jody led Jeremy to the garage. Mr. Ewing was there,

working on his prototype grass carpet. "Well, what have we here?" he asked when he saw the children.

"I'm blind," Jeremy said. "This is Jody, my seeing-eye dog."

"Woof!" Jody barked.

"But you know I'm allergic to dogs," Mr. Ewing said. He pretended to sneeze.

"Okay, she's not a dog," Jeremy decided. "She's a pig! She's even smarter than a dog. And no long hair to make you sneeze."

"Oink, oink," Jody squealed. She pressed the tip of her nose with her finger to make it look like a snout. "Miss Piggy, move over!" She giggled.

But Mr. Ewing wasn't laughing. He was staring into space with a faraway look in his eyes. Slowly, his eyebrows lifted and three deep wrinkles formed across his forehead.

"Well, well, well," he said in a husky voice. "Why not? They're smart, they're friendly. And for blind people who are allergic to dogs . . ." His voice trailed off.

Jeremy opened his eyes. "Daddy, what are you talking about?"

"Kids, I'm through with job hunting," Mr. Ewing announced. "I don't want to work for anyone else ever again."

"You mean you're going to open a store and sell your inventions?" Jody asked eagerly.

"Not exactly. What I've got in mind isn't an invention per se. Actually, it's more of a scheme. It involves the whole family, too."

"Oh, boy!" Jody exclaimed. "What is it, Daddy?"

Mr. Ewing folded his arms across his chest and grinned. "The Ewing family is going to train the world's first seeing-eye pigs!"

Chapter Three

When the school bus stopped, Jody jumped off and ran down the street like a sprinter on the way to the finish line. Today was a very special day. For starters, it was the last day of the school year and the beginning of summer vacation. But even more importantly, it was the day her family was moving to a small farm in Yellow Bluff, Kansas, to train seeing-eye pigs.

Jody's heart beat faster when she saw the big orange moving truck parked in her driveway. Her mother was standing beside it, calling out instructions to the movers. "Be careful with that table," she warned. "It's a one-of-a-kind."

"I can see that, lady." The moving man chuckled as he hoisted the family's bumpy, oddly shaped dining room table into the truck.

"When are we leaving?" Jody asked, running up to join her mom.

"Any minute. Better check your room and make sure you haven't forgotten anything."

Jody went into the house. Her bedroom was empty

except for a stack of cardboard boxes piled in the middle of the floor. She checked the closets. They were empty, too. She tried an experimental cartwheel across the bare floor, then sat down and looked around.

Jody had read books about kids whose family moved to a new town. In the stories, the kids always felt sad to leave their old house. But Jody didn't feel sad at all. To her, moving was as natural as breathing. Her family did it every year or so, each time her father started a new job. In the last three years alone they'd lived in Pennsylvania, Delaware, and Baltimore, Maryland.

Still, this time was going to be different. For once, her father wasn't going to be working at a job he hated. Instead, he was going to be working for himself, doing something he really cared about. If he succeeded, Jody told herself, people would finally stop calling him a kook. But if he failed . . . Jody shuddered. She didn't want to think about that.

"Jody?"

She looked up to find Jeremy standing in the doorway. In his hands was the mason jar with Rosie the garden slug inside. "Ready to go?" she asked.

"I guess so," he answered uncertainly. "Can I take Rosie?"

"Sure. Why not?"

Jeremy gazed into the jar with a worried frown. "Maybe she won't like Kansas."

Jody wondered if Jeremy felt worried, too. "I think we're all going to like Kansas," she said. "Just think about it. Daddy isn't going to be working at a regular job anymore. We'll all be working together, training baby pigs."

"Can I have one for a pet?" Jeremy asked.

17

"They'll all be our pets," Jody replied. "And Rosie will be your pet, too."

"Hear that, Rosie?" Jeremy said to his slug. "Kansas is going to be fun."

Jody smiled. By making Jeremy feel better, she had made herself feel better, too. Suddenly, she felt certain her father wasn't going to fail. Eagerly, she took her little brother's hand and skipped outside. She could hardly wait to get to Kansas!

Out in the front yard, Jody and Jeremy found Dwight helping their father pack the family car, a beat-up old station wagon that the kids had painted with rainbow-colored stripes. Mr. Ewing squeezed a potted plant into the last bit of empty space and announced, "Looks like we're all set."

"So long," Mrs. Ewing called to the movers. "See you in Yellow Bluff three days from now."

Mr. Ewing closed the car door and walked to the AirStream trailer that was attached to the car's rear fender. Mr. Ewing had bought the trailer last week from an elderly couple across town. It was shiny silver with rounded corners and tiny windows. It looked like a spaceship from an old science fiction movie. "Hop in, kids," he said with a smile. "Our adventure is about to begin!"

Jody, Dwight, and Jeremy climbed into the trailer. The floor was covered with the world's first wall-to-wall grass carpet, designed and installed by Mr. Ewing. Jody took off her shoes and let her toes sink into the cool grass. Heavenly!

Mrs. Ewing climbed into the trailer with the kids and closed the door. Then Mr. Ewing got in the station wagon and drove away from the house, pulling the trailer behind. Dwight, Jody, and Jeremy crowded

18

around the trailer's tiny back windows, watching their house get smaller and smaller. Soon it was just a tiny speck in the distance, and then Mr. Ewing turned the corner and it disappeared altogether.

Jody turned from the window and let out a cheer. They were on their way!

Three days later, the family was still driving. They had traveled through the mountains of West Virginia, across the grassy hills of Kentucky, and over the wide Mississippi River. Now they were rumbling across eastern Kansas, on their way to Yellow Bluff.

Mrs. Ewing was sitting at the kitchenette table, reading a book about the plants and wildlife of Kansas. "Did you know the Kansas state flower is the native sunflower?" she said to no one in particular. "If there aren't any of those growing around our new house, I'm going to plant some."

Dwight nodded just to be polite, but the truth was he couldn't have cared less about sunflowers or anything else that had to do with Kansas. As far as he was concerned, the whole seeing-eye pig scheme was just plain goofy. There was no reason to believe pigs could be trained, and anyway, who would want to? Besides, there was no money in it. *The only way to make money from pigs*, he thought, *is to turn them into pork chops*.

Dwight turned a page in the book he was reading, *How to Make a Million Before You Turn Twenty-One*. He had convinced his parents to let him invest the fifty dollars from his piggybank in pork belly futures, and now he was spending every spare minute learning about the commodities market. He was determined he wasn't going to lose a penny of his money—especially since his parents said if he didn't turn a profit by the end of

19

the summer, he had to get a part-time job and earn back everything he lost.

Jody was lying on one of the cushioned benches, daydreaming about Kansas. All she knew about the midwest was what she had read in books by Laura Ingalls Wilder like *Little House on the Prairie*. She wondered if she and her family would live in a log cabin and hunt deer with rifles like Laura's family.

"Hey, Jody," Jeremy said, walking over and tugging at her sleeve, "read me a book."

"Not the *The Three Little Pigs* again," Jody moaned. "I'm so sick of that story."

"Then what about *Pig William*?" Jeremy suggested.

"Why don't you read it to me? I'm sure by now you must know it by heart."

While Jeremy went to get the book, Jody closed her eyes and went back to her daydreaming. She imagined herself wearing a long flowered dress and riding in a horse and buggy. Suddenly, some dangerous bandits rode their horses over the hill. "Give us all your money or we'll blow you full of buckshot!" the head bandit said, pointing his rifle at Jody. Little did they know that she always carried a miniature pistol in her purse. With a sly smile, she reached inside and—

"We're here!" Mrs. Ewing exclaimed.

Jody opened her eyes with a start. "Where?" she asked.

"Yellow Bluff," Mrs. Ewing said.

"Oh, boy!" Jody jumped up and peered out the window, half-expecting to see bandits riding their horses alongside the trailer. Instead, she saw a bumpy, two-lane highway with wheat fields stretching out to the horizon on either side. Soon the trailer turned down a long, dirt driveway lined with trees.

"These are the first trees I've seen in miles," Dwight remarked.

"And they're ours," Mrs. Ewing said.

"You mean—"

"Yes, this is our farm. Didn't you see the address on the mailbox out by the road? 4323 Yellow Bluff Highway. And look, there's our . . ."

Mrs. Ewing's voice trailed off as the house came into view. It was a white, two-story wooden farmhouse with black shutters—a beautiful old place except for one thing. Most of the roof was missing!

"Where's the top of the house?" Jeremy asked.

"I . . . I don't know," Mrs. Ewing said with dismay. "The real-estate agent in Baltimore showed us photographs and it looked fine. I mean, it definitely had a roof when we bought it."

The trailer bounced to a stop and Mrs. Ewing jumped out, followed by Jody, Dwight, and Jeremy. They joined Mr. Ewing, who was standing beside the station wagon with his hands on his hips, staring up at the top of the house.

"It looks like the whale skeleton we saw in the aquarium in Baltimore," Jody said, pointing to the ridgepole that still ran across the peak of the roof and the five or six rafters that rested against it. "See, there's the backbone and some ribs."

"That's the frame," Mr. Ewing said. "Or what's left of it."

"But what happened to the rest of the roof?" Dwight asked impatiently.

"Tornado," said a deep voice behind them.

The whole family spun around. There was a black pickup truck parked behind their trailer. A beefy man in overalls and a green cap was sitting in it, chewing on a wad of tobacco.

"Howdy, folks," he said, tipping his hat. "Welcome to Yellow Bluff. Name's Henry Bruder. I own the farm across the road. Don't mean to intrude, but I saw you turn into the driveway and I said to myself, 'There's them folks from back east that come to live in the old Turner place.' "

"Yes, that's us," Mr. Ewing said. "But what happened to the roof? Did you say—?"

"Yep, tornado. One come through last week. Tore right across my wheat field and then headed straight for your house. You're lucky it didn't do worse. I've seen a tornado pick a house right up, carry it a couple of miles, and then drop it down on someone else's land."

"Just like in *The Wizard of Oz*," Jody said with awe.

"That's right," Mr. Bruder said with a nod. "Anyway, just want you to know you're welcome to stay at our place tonight if you need to."

"Thank you," Mrs. Ewing said, "but I think we'll be all right. We can sleep in our trailer until we get the roof fixed."

"Okeydokey," Mr. Bruder said. He glanced at Dwight. "By the way, son, how old are you?"

"Thirteen," Dwight answered.

"Same age as my boy, Charlie. You two'll have to get together. There's a 4-H meeting coming up soon. I'll tell Charlie to let you know when and where." He tipped his hat. "Well, so long, folks. If I can be of any help, just give a holler." With that, he put his truck in gear and drove off down the driveway.

"Dwight, isn't that lucky there's a boy your age nearby?" Mr. Ewing said with a smile.

"I guess," Dwight said. "What's 4-H?"

"It's a club for kids who are interested in farming," Mr. Ewing explained.

Dwight rolled his eyes. "Come on, Dad, I don't want to hang out with a bunch of farmers. They're probably total hicks."

"Dwight . . ." Mr. Ewing began.

"Look, I'm sure they're nice and all. But dirty overalls and chewing tobacco are not exactly my idea of cool."

"Can we talk about this later?" Mrs. Ewing broke in. "In case you've forgotten, we have a house without a roof. What are we going to do when the movers show up? We've got to put the furniture someplace."

"Yes, well, you're right," Mr. Ewing said thoughtfully. Then slowly, his eyebrows lifted, and three deep wrinkles formed across his forehead. "Of course we could . . . for the time being anyway . . . well, why not?"

"What?" Jody asked eagerly.

"You'll see," Mr. Ewing said with a mysterious smile. He squinted up at the sun. "Nice weather, isn't it? I heard on the radio it's supposed to last at least a couple more weeks." He glanced down at his watch. "Well, the movers should be showing up soon. Until they do, let's look around."

Next to the house was a faded red barn. In front of it was another wooden building with a fenced-in dirt yard. "Is that where the pigs are going to live?" Jody asked.

"That's right," Mr. Ewing replied. "That's the pigpen, and behind it are stalls for the pigs to go into when it's cold or rainy."

"Are there pigs in there now?" Jeremy asked hopefully.

"No. I ordered ten baby mini-pigs from a breeder in Nebraska. They're arriving tomorrow on the one o'clock train."

"Ten pigs!" Dwight exclaimed. "But Dad, we don't even know for sure that pigs can be trained. Why don't we just start with one and see how things work out?"

"Because pigs have personalities, just like people," Mr. Ewing said. "Some are smarter than others, some are better-behaved, and so on. Out of ten mini-pigs maybe only one or two will be good candidates for seeing-eye training. We have to test them and find out."

"What's the difference between a pig and a mini-pig?" Jody asked.

"A normal pig can weigh up to 1,200 pounds," Mr. Ewing explained, "but mini-pigs are bred to weigh only about 100 pounds—just the perfect size for a house pet."

"Or a seeing-eye pig," Mrs. Ewing added.

While they were talking, the moving van rumbled up the driveway. The men got out and stared up at the roofless house with their mouths hanging open. "I'm telling you right now, buddy," the driver said, "we ain't carrying anything upstairs."

"But—" Mr. Ewing began.

"It's in our contract. We don't have to enter any structure that looks unsafe. And that second floor is definitely unsafe!"

"But that's fine," Mr. Ewing said calmly. "We don't want the bedroom furniture inside. We want it right here, on the front lawn."

"What?" the driver gasped.

"What?" Mrs. Ewing and the children cried.

"It will be like camping," Mr. Ewing explained, "only with all the comforts of home."

"Whatever you say, buddy," the driver said, shaking his head. "Okay, boys, start unloading."

While the Ewings watched, the moving men unloaded all the living room, dining room, and kitchen furniture and carried it into the house. After that, they unloaded the bedroom furniture and spread it out across the front lawn. Then they got in their truck and drove away, still shaking their heads in amazement.

When the moving men were gone, the Ewings went inside their trailer and ate dinner. Later, when it was time for bed, they changed into their pajamas and walked out onto their new lawn. Their beds were spread out across the grass, along with all their dressers, chairs, lamps, and boxes of clothes.

"What did I tell you?" Mr. Ewing said after they'd all crawled into bed. "Just like camping, only better, right?"

"Wow!" Dwight exclaimed. "Look at all those stars!"

Jody rolled on her back and gazed up at the sky. She had never seen so many stars before. There seemed to be billions of them, twinkling down at her like Christmas lights.

Jody smiled. She had been wrong about Kansas, she realized. She was going to live in a two-story farmhouse, not a log cabin. She would be training pigs, not hunting for food with a rifle. And there were no bandits in sight.

But she didn't mind. Camping in her own bed in the middle of her new front lawn was just as much fun as

anything Laura Ingalls Wilder had ever done, she was
sure of it. And who knew what tomorrow might bring?
New places to explore, new adventures, maybe even
new friends. With a sigh, she closed her eyes and fell
into a deep, contented sleep.

Chapter Four

Dwight woke up the next morning with the sun on his face and dew on his pillow. He threw back the covers and stretched. Birds were singing in the trees and somewhere in the distance, a rooster was crowing. His family was still asleep, so he got up quietly and went into the new house to look around.

The first floor hadn't been touched by the tornado. There was a spacious living room with high ceilings and a big fireplace, a dining room with a glass chandelier, and a kitchen with a huge pantry. The second floor, however, was a disaster. Wood, plaster, and roofing tiles were lying all over the floors. There were gaping holes in the ceiling, and when Dwight looked up he could see patches of sky.

What a mess, he thought. He stepped over a pile of plaster and looked out a window that faced onto the back of the house. He saw a flat, unplowed field covered with tall grass and wildflowers. Beyond that, fields of golden wheat stretched off to the horizon. Far in the distance, he could see the house and barn of another farm. He estimated they were almost a mile away.

Dwight walked into the bathroom and looked out of the small window over the sink. He was facing the front of the house now. Yesterday Mr. Bruder had told them that his farm was across the road. Dwight stood on tiptoe and tried to see it, but his view was blocked by the trees that lined the Ewings' driveway.

Dwight groaned. He was used to living in the suburbs, surrounded by other houses with lots of kids. *This is the middle of nowhere,* he thought with disgust.

"What're you looking at?"

Dwight spun around to find his father standing at the door of the bathroom, smiling at him. "Nothing," he said. After all, he figured, that's exactly what was out there. Nothing. "Dad," he asked, "how much of the land behind the house is ours?"

"Only that one unplowed field. The real-estate agent told us the farm used to be much bigger. But when the last owners retired, they sold off most of the land to the Bruders."

Dwight thought it over. If they had to live on this boring old farm, he decided, at least they should be making some money from it. "You should hire someone to farm what's left," he said.

"I don't think your mother would like that. She loves wildflowers."

"But you can't make money off of wildflowers," Dwight said. "Now if you planted some wheat . . ."

"Why don't *you* farm it?" Mr. Ewing suggested.

Dwight flicked a piece of lint off his cuff. "Me? I don't know anything about farming." *And I don't want to, either,* he thought.

"But you could learn. I'll bet the 4-H Club has lots of information."

"No, thanks," Dwight said with a laugh. "There's more money in the commodites market. And you don't have to dig around in the dirt to make it."

"This is it?" Dwight asked incredulously as the Ewings drove down the narrow main street of Yellow Bluff that afternoon.

"This is downtown Yellow Bluff," Mr. Ewing replied, slowing down as a pickup truck loaded with caged chickens turned in front of them. "Why? Is something wrong?"

"Well, it's just so . . . so small." Dwight read the signs on the passing stores—Ed's Barbershop, Baum's Farm Supply, the Hoedown Tavern. "I haven't seen one video arcade or comic-book store," he complained. "And where's the Cineplex?"

"I doubt they have one," Mrs. Ewing said. "But look at that." She pointed to an old-fashioned movie theater with a neon marquee. "They don't make them like that anymore."

And I'm glad they don't, Dwight thought. The place looked as if it was crumbling apart. Besides, there was only one movie showing, and it was one he had seen weeks ago back in Baltimore.

Dwight rested his head against the back of the seat and sighed. Sure, his father had said Yellow Bluff was a small town, but Dwight still hadn't been prepared for *this.* Not one of the buildings on the main street was taller than two stories. There were no department stores and only one small grocery store. And where were all the people? There were only five or six cars on the street, and the sidewalks were almost completely empty.

29

But maybe that wasn't all that surprising, Dwight decided, considering that the time-and-temperature sign in front of the Prairie Savings and Loan read 102 degrees.

"I'm hungry," Jeremy said.

"Me, too," Jody chimed in.

"Let's find a restaurant," Mr. Ewing suggested. "We've got an hour before the train's due."

"There's one," Mrs. Ewing said, pointing out the window to a little restaurant called Elsie's Cafe.

Mr. Ewing parked the station wagon, and the family trooped into the restaurant. The place looked like something out of an old black-and-white movie—tin ceilings, scuffed linoleum floors, worn wooden booths, and a long counter with stools. The people looked old-fashioned, too. There were farmers in muddy overalls, businessmen with suspenders and loosened ties, and mothers with apple-cheeked babies. The waitresses wore pink uniforms and hair nets, and they seemed to be calling all the customers by name.

As the Ewings made their way through the restaurant, everyone turned to stare at them. Some people even leaned over to whisper to their neighbors. Dwight could feel the back of his neck turning red. He overheard a few whispered words as he walked along—"strangers," "old Turner place," and "city folk." How embarrassing! He wished he could turn around and leave.

But Mr. Ewing didn't seem to notice. He took a seat in the empty booth and smiled at everyone who glanced his way. "Looks like a friendly bunch," he said to Mrs. Ewing.

"Afternoon, folks," the waitress said, tossing a stack of menus on the table. She was a middle-aged woman with a mass of curly blonde hair held in place with a

30

hair net, and huge, red hoop earrings. "Just passing through?"

"No," Mr. Ewing replied, "we live here. We bought the Turner farm out on Yellow Bluff Highway."

Dwight glanced around the room. Everyone was leaning forward in their chairs to hear what his father was saying.

"Well, welcome, then," the waitress said. "I'm Elsie, and you've just walked into the best restaurant in town. In fact, it's the *only* restaurant in town." She chuckled merrily and went to get glasses of water. "What are you planning on doing out at the old Turner place?" she asked when she returned. "Farming?"

"No. I'm not a farmer," Mr. Ewing said. "I'm sort of . . . well . . ."

"An idea man," Jody finished.

Mr. Ewing laughed. "Well, yes, I guess I am. Anyway, I came up with an interesting theory, and I decided to move my family out here to test it out. We're going to train seeing-eye pigs."

The whole room burst out laughing. Mr. Ewing looked startled, but then he laughed, too. "It sounds crazy, I know," he said, addressing the room, "but think about it. Pigs are smart. Smarter than dogs, some say. And for blind people who are allergic to dogs . . . well, it's a natural."

"You can't train pigs to do nothing," a chubby man in overalls protested loudly. "They're too stubborn."

"And filthy," another farmer added.

"Ah, but that's a fallacy," Mr. Ewing replied. "Actually, pigs are quite clean . . ."

"Oh, yeah?" the chubby man said. "Well, I wish you'd stop by my farm and tell my pigs that. They seem to think they're supposed to wallow in mud all day."

Everyone laughed, but Mr. Ewing just smiled good-naturedly. "Pigs are very intelligent," he said. "For example, they can swim and they can learn to do tricks."

"I don't care if my pigs can do the Sunday crossword puzzle," the chubby farmer said. "They're still only good for one thing. Bacon!"

"Well, maybe you're right," Mr. Ewing said. "But just a few years ago, no one would have thought you could teach a gorilla to talk. Now there are gorillas who speak sign language."

"You planning on teaching your pigs to talk?" a woman in a flowered dress asked.

"Next thing you know, he'll be telling us our cows can do arithmetic and our chickens can speak Spanish!" the chubby man said. The whole room guffawed loudly.

"Okay, okay," Elsie broke in, "I haven't got all day, you know. Let these good people order, will ya?" She took a pencil from behind her ear and said, "What can I get for you, folks? A ham sandwich?" She burst out laughing and the whole room joined in.

Finally, things calmed down enough for the Ewings to order lunch. The food was fabulous—crispy fried chicken, french fries, and coleslaw—but Dwight was too miserable to care. Why did his father have to be such a blabbermouth? he wondered unhappily. If only his dad had lied a little and said he was planning to farm the land, no one would have laughed at him. But no, he had to tell everyone about his seeing-eye pig scheme. And now the whole town thought he was nuts.

Dwight picked at his coleslaw. Out of the corner of his eye, he noticed someone walking to the cash register. It was Mr. Bruder. Walking beside him was a husky boy about Dwight's age with straight, straw-colored hair.

Mr. Ewing saw them, too. "Mr. Bruder," he called cheerfully. "How are you?"

"Hello, folks," Mr. Bruder said, coming over to the booth. "That's quite an idea you have—seeing-eye pigs." He chuckled and shook his head. "I wish you luck."

"Is this your son?" Mrs. Ewing asked.

"Yep, this is my boy, Charlie."

"And this is Dwight," Mrs. Ewing said.

Mr. Bruder turned to his son. "I told Dwight you'd take him along to a 4-H meeting sometime."

Charlie made a face. "Do I have to?"

"Now, Charlie . . ."

"But he's a city kid. I bet he doesn't know the first thing about farming."

"That's enough, young man," Mr. Bruder said in a warning tone. He turned to Mr. Ewing. "So, what are your plans for the house? Have you hired anyone to fix the roof yet?"

While the rest of the family talked about the new house, Charlie leaned over to Dwight and said, "Seeing-eye pigs, huh? What's the matter, couldn't your father get a real job?"

Dwight scowled with embarrassment. It was only a matter of time before every kid in town would be asking the same thing. He'd never hear the end of it. If only he could come up with some way to make them forget his father's loony seeing-eye pig scheme. Something that would impress them and make them like him. But what?

Then, all at once, he had an idea. It was so perfect, he could hardly keep from grinning. Before he could

33

chicken out, he turned to Charlie and said, "Actually, my dad already has a real job."

"Oh, yeah? What is it? Teaching horses to tap-dance?"

"Very funny. Look, I'm not supposed to say anything about this. So if I tell you, you've got to promise to keep it a secret."

Now Charlie looked interested. "What?"

"Promise you won't tell?"

"Okay, I promise. What's the big secret?"

Dwight motioned Charlie closer and whispered in his ear. "My family is rich."

"Yeah, sure." Charlie laughed. "And my dad is president of the United States."

"No, I mean it," Dwight whispered. "My father is an investor. He's made millions in the stock market. He just bought this farm as a tax write-off."

"Are you serious?"

"Absolutely. But don't tell anyone. If people knew we were rich, they'd treat us special. But Dad doesn't want that. He brought us to Kansas so we could see how ordinary people live."

"Wow! But that still doesn't explain the seeing-eye pigs."

"If we don't lose money on the farm, Dad can't write it off his taxes. So he came up with the seeing-eye pig idea." Dwight shrugged. "Can you think of a better way to lose money?"

"Man," Charlie said in an awestruck voice, "your dad is really smart."

Dwight smiled modestly. But inside, he was grinning. Okay, so maybe he'd told a couple of white lies. The important thing was that Charlie was really impressed. That meant he wouldn't make fun of the Ewings again. Dwight picked up a piece of fried chicken and took a big bite. For the first time since he'd moved to Yellow Bluff, he felt terrific.

Chapter Five

The Yellow Bluff train station was easy to find. It was right next to the tallest building in town, a forty-foot-high grain silo. The Ewings drove up beside it just as the one o'clock freight train pulled into the station.

As soon as the train chugged to a stop, the stationmaster came out of the station. While he filled out some forms, three workmen in brown coveralls began unloading bags of feed from one of the boxcars.

"Excuse me, uh . . . Mr. Harrigan," Mr. Ewing said, reading the name tag on the stationmaster's blue suit. "I'm here to pick up ten mini-pigs."

"Ah, yes," Mr. Harrigan replied, lifting his bushy eyebrows. "Come with me."

The Ewings followed the stationmaster to a long brown boxcar. He opened the door, and there they were—ten pink piglets in ten heavy wood-and-wire crates. As the sunlight hit their faces, they pressed their noses against the wire and squealed excitedly.

"Sign here," Mr. Harrigan said, thrusting a clipboard in front of Mr. Ewing. Then he picked up the crates and began heaving them carelessly onto the platform. The pigs shrieked loudly.

"Stop!" Jeremy cried. "You're scaring them!" He knelt down beside the cages and spoke softly to the piglets. "It's okay. We're not going to hurt you. We're your friends."

One of the pigs pressed his nose against the wire and grunted softly. He was smaller than the other pigs. He had pale brown spots on his face and a cut on one of his ears. Jeremy put his fingers through the wire and touched the piglet's nose. The pig grunted happily and licked Jeremy's fingers.

"These crates are too big to fit in our car," Mrs. Ewing said to Mr. Harrigan. "Do you have anything smaller?"

"Sorry, lady," he said as he started back up the platform. "All we do is deliver the pigs. After that, it's up to you."

"What now?" Dwight asked his parents.

"I'll pull the station wagon closer," Mr. Ewing said. "Then we'll take the pigs out of the crates and put them in the back of the car."

"Without the crates?" Mrs. Ewing asked uncertainly.

"Don't worry," Jeremy said eagerly. "I'll sit in the back and hold them in my lap."

"Me, too," Jody said.

"You sure they won't want to run around?" Dwight asked.

"Look at them," Mr. Ewing said, pointing to the pigs. They had quieted down and were lying peacefully in their cages. "The poor little things are worn out from the train ride. They'll probably huddle in a corner and fall asleep."

The crates were nailed shut, so Dwight borrowed a

crowbar from the workmen. As he pried open the first crate—the one that contained the piglet with the cut on his ear—all the pigs began to wag their tails and snort eagerly.

Dwight lifted off the top of the crate and picked up the little piglet, who let out an excited squeal and squirmed in his arms. Dwight hugged the piglet tighter and started for the station wagon. But as he stepped off the platform onto the grass, the piglet began to squirm and grunt with delight. "Hey, pig, knock it off!" Dwight cried.

"Don't let him get loose," Jody warned, hurrying forward to help. Too late. With an ecstatic shriek, the piglet kicked Dwight in the stomach and wiggled out of his arms. Then he ran to the grass and began to roll in it.

"Grab him!" Mrs. Ewing cried. The whole family rushed toward the piglet. Instantly, the little pig jumped to his feet and started running.

"After him!" Mr. Ewing shouted. "Hurry!"

The piglet ran across the grass and hopped onto the platform, swerving back and forth like a football player on his way to score a touchdown. Once, Jody managed to grab his tail, but he wiggled away before she could get her arms around him. Another time Mr. Ewing tried to tackle the pig, but he missed and landed on his stomach in the middle of the platform.

Up ahead, Mr. Harrigan was helping the workers unload the last of the bags of feed. The piglet ran between his legs and behind the stack of bags. Mr. Harrigan lost his balance and fell on the bags. They toppled over and one ripped open. With a joyful grunt, the piglet began gobbling up the loose feed.

"Hey, that's not for you!" Mr. Harrigan cried.

"That's chicken feed." He grabbed the piglet by the ears and dragged him away from the food.

"Stop!" Jeremy shouted, running up. "You're hurting him!"

"Hurting *him*?" Mr. Harrigan gasped, crawling to his knees and grabbing the pig tightly in his arms. "What about me? And what about this bag of feed?"

"We're terribly sorry," Mr. Ewing said. "We'll pay for any damages we've caused. Now, if we can just have our pig . . ."

The stationmaster handed the squirming piglet over to Mr. Ewing. "That's the last of those pigs—and you—I ever want to see again. Good-bye!"

"Guess this little guy wasn't quite as sleepy as you thought," Mrs. Ewing said, reaching over to pat the wiggling piglet.

"That's a baby for you." Mr. Ewing chuckled, hurrying down the platform with the piglet in his arms. "Our kids never slept when we wanted them to, either."

"Did we squeal like little pigs?" Jeremy asked.

"Louder," Mrs. Ewing said with a laugh.

When they reached the station wagon, Jody and Jeremy got in the back. Dwight put the runaway piglet in with them. Immediately, the pig began running in circles around the back of the station wagon, leaping over Jody and Jeremy as he went. The children giggled and tried to catch him. But the piglet only ran faster, squealing with joy at this exciting new game.

"Okay, let's get the rest of them," Mr. Ewing said. "Only this time we'll carry the crates to the station wagon before we open them."

Soon the back of the station wagon was filled with pigs. They chased each other around and around, nipping at one another's tails and squealing loudly. "Drive fast," Mrs. Ewing said as she got in the car. "I don't think I can stand this for very long."

Mr. Ewing put the station wagon in reverse and pulled out of the parking lot. The pigs responded by squealing even louder. One of them jumped into the backseat and hopped on Dwight's lap. "Hey, get off of me!" Dwight cried. He tried to grab the piglet and return it to the back of the station wagon, but the pig wiggled away and slid off the seat to the floor.

"Oh-oh," Jody said. "One of them just went to the bathroom."

"Ew!" Dwight moaned. "It stinks!"

"Don't open the window," Mr. Ewing warned. "They might jump out."

"Dumb pigs," Dwight complained.

"It's not their fault," Jeremy said. "They're scared. I bet they never rode in a car before."

"And they never will again," Mrs. Ewing said. "Not if I have anything to do with it!"

It was a long ride home—or at least it seemed that way to the Ewings. But finally Mr. Ewing turned down the narrow, tree-lined driveway and pulled up in front of their farmhouse.

"Air!" Dwight cried, throwing open the car door. "I'm suffocating!"

Instantly, the pig who had slid to the floor leaped up and ran out the door. The other piglets hopped into the backseat and followed. They took off across the front lawn, running among the family's beds. One of the pigs—a skinny one with long ears—began rooting in the grass with his snout. The little piglet with the cut on his ear wiggled under Mr. and Mrs. Ewing's bed. Another pig—the biggest and fattest of the brood—

40

chased after him, nipping at his tail. Still another grabbed Dwight's blanket in his mouth and trotted across the yard with it.

"Hey, put that down!" Dwight cried. He jumped out of the station wagon and ran after the pig. The animal dropped the blanket and took off in the direction of the Airstream trailer. He waddled up the steps and pushed open the unlocked door.

"No!" gasped Mrs. Ewing, leaping out of the car. "They can't go in there!"

Dwight followed the piglet into the trailer. Three more curious piglets ran after him. Mrs. Ewing followed them all. The piglets ran through the trailer, pausing long enough to root in the wall-to-wall grass carpet, wiggle under the benches, and finish off a half-eaten bag of M&M's that was lying on the table. Dwight and Mrs. Ewing chased after them, slapping the pigs on their rumps and shouting, "Go on! Get out of here! Now!"

The confused pigs finally got the idea and ran out of the trailer. Dwight and Mrs. Ewing jogged after them. Out on the lawn, they found Jody, Jeremy, and Mr. Ewing chasing the rest of the piglets around the yard. The humans looked tired and frazzled, but the pigs were still filled with energy. They ran over, under, and around the beds, grunting giddily.

"Wait a minute!" Mrs. Ewing called. "This is ridiculous. We can't catch pigs this way."

"Have you got a better idea?" Mr. Ewing panted.

"Yes." She headed for the house. "I'll be right back." When she reappeared, she was carrying a bucket filled to the brim with something that looked like Mishmash Surprise. "Here, piggy, piggy, piggy," she called, swinging the bucket invitingly.

41

The piglets took one whiff of the food and stopped in their tracks. Their snouts twitched eagerly. Then they chased after Mrs. Ewing. Within seconds, she was surrounded by a pack of grunting, squirming pigs.

"That's right," she said, making her way slowly toward the pigpen. "Follow me. Good piggies."

Mr. Ewing hurried over to the fenced-in pen and opened the gate. Mrs. Ewing walked inside, followed by the piglets. She emptied the bucket of food into the pig trough. The pigs made a beeline for it and began noisily slurping it up.

Mrs. Ewing slipped through the gate and locked it behind her. The whole family surrounded her and let out a cheer. "Good thinking, Mommy," Jeremy said.

"You were terrific," Mr. Ewing agreed, giving her a kiss on the cheek.

Dwight had recovered his blanket from the lawn. It was covered with grass stains and ripped in two or three places. Jody took it out of his hands and draped it over her mother's shoulders. "For bravery beyond the call of duty," she announced importantly. "You are now a member of the Royal Order of Wild Piggies. Rise, Sir Mom."

Mrs. Ewing laughed. "You know," she said, "I think we learned something important today."

"You have to be nuts to want to raise pigs?" Dwight suggested.

"That could be." She chuckled. "But I was thinking of something else. The way to a pig's heart is through his stomach."

"What was in that bucket, Mom?" Jody asked.

"Leftover chocolate-chip pancakes, some potato chips, baked beans, a head of lettuce . . . and the hamburgers we were going to eat for dinner tonight."

"Oh, Mom!" Jody moaned.

Mrs. Ewing pushed a few messy hairs out of her eyes. "Guess we'll just have to go back to Elsie's Cafe. But right now dinner is the furthest thing from my mind." She walked wearily across the lawn and sat on her bed. "I need a rest. Those pigs wore me out."

Jody followed and flopped down on her own bed. Suddenly, the sheet started to move and a pink ear popped out from under the pillow. Jody let out a scream and leaped up. "Mom!" she cried, "there's a pig in my bed!"

It was the little piglet with the cut on his ear. In the midst of all the excitement, he had wiggled under the covers and fallen asleep. Now he hopped to his feet and looked around nervously as if to say, *What happened to all my buddies?*

"Poor little guy," Jeremy said, running over and sitting on the edge of the bed. He put his fingers up to the piglet's snout. The pig sniffed and licked them. Then he grunted happily and crawled into Jeremy's lap.

"I think you've found a friend," Mrs. Ewing said.

"I'm going to call him Willy," Jeremy said, "after Wilbur in *Charlotte's Web.*"

Mr. Ewing smiled and nodded. "Willy it is."

Jeremy spent the rest of the afternoon playing with Willy. He discovered that if he crawled around the yard on his hands and knees, Willy would follow him. They were still playing follow the leader when dinnertime rolled around. "Time to go to Elsie's," Mr. Ewing called from the porch. "Put Willy back in his pen."

Jeremy picked Willy up and placed him inside the pigpen. Immediately, the biggest pig of the group trotted over and gave Willy a shove with his snout. Willy

43

let out a frightened squeal and ran behind the food trough.

"Stop that, you stinker," Jeremy scolded, wagging his finger at the fat pig. Then he hurried to join his family in the station wagon. "You know the cut on Willy's ear?" he said as he climbed in the back. "I bet that big, fat pig bit him. Did you see him chasing Willy around the lawn when we first brought them home?"

"Yeah," Jody said. "That fat one was biting all the others in the car, too. He's a real Rambo."

"Now we've named two pigs," Mr. Ewing said. "Willy and Rambo."

Later, after a dinner of melt-in-your-mouth pot roast and mashed potatoes at Elsie's Cafe, the family returned home. As soon as Mr. Ewing stopped the car, Jeremy jumped out and headed for the pigpen. Willy was at the trough, trying to eat some of the pig feed that Mr. Ewing had put out earlier. But as he leaned down for a bite, Rambo pushed him aside with his snout. Willy tried again, but Rambo huffed angrily and nipped the little one's tail.

"Poor Willy," Jeremy said. He knelt down beside the fence. "Come here, boy. Come on."

"Don't take that pig out of the pen again," Mrs. Ewing called. "It's almost your bedtime and you need a shower."

"But Mom, Rambo won't let Willy eat."

"Well, I'm sorry, but Willy's going to have to learn to take care of himself. That's part of being a piglet. Now march into the motor home and turn on the water."

Jeremy did as he was told. But later, when he was tucked into his bed beneath the stars, he felt an overwhelming temptation to see how Willy was doing. The

44

rest of the family was inside the motor home, so Jeremy put on his glasses and tiptoed over to the pigpen. "Willy, where are you?" he whispered, staring into the darkness.

A moment later, the little piglet with the cut on his ear appeared at the fence. "Hello, little guy," Jeremy said. "Is Rambo giving you a hard time?"

Willy grunted and pushed his snout between the railings of the fence. Jeremy frowned. He wished he could do something to help Willy out. But what? Then suddenly, he had a wonderful idea. He glanced toward the motor home to make sure the coast was clear. Then he opened the gate. Willy let out an oink and ran gratefully into his arms. "Come on, buddy," Jeremy whispered. "I'll take you someplace where there aren't any bullies."

Jeremy walked to his bed and got in. Willy lay down beside him. "Good boy," Jeremy said. "You're hungry, aren't you?"

Willy snorted and licked Jeremy's fingers. "I thought so." Jeremy reached into the pocket of his pajamas. Inside were some mint candies he'd gotten from a bowl beside the cash register at Elsie's Cafe. "Here you go, boy. Try these."

Willy gobbled down the mints like a vacuum cleaner sucking up dust balls. Then he snuggled close to Jeremy and closed his eyes. "Good boy," Jeremy whispered. He took off his glasses and let his head fall back onto the pillow. Before long, he and Willy were both fast asleep.

Chapter Six

After breakfast the next morning, Mr. Ewing pushed back his chair and said, "Today we're going to test the pigs to find out which ones will make the best seeing-eye guides."

"How do we do that?" Jody asked.

Mr. Ewing took a pamphlet out of the back pocket of his jeans. The title was *Training Guide Dogs for the Blind*. "I ordered this from an organization in California that trains seeing-eye dogs. It explains all the basic rules for selecting and training dogs."

"But will it work for pigs?" Dwight asked.

"That's what we're going to find out."

Mr. Ewing led the family out to the pigpen. As soon as the piglets saw him, they ran to the fence, snorting enthusiastically.

"Here, Willy," Jeremy called, kneeling down beside the fence. The little piglet with the cut on his ear squirmed past the other pigs to get close to Jeremy. "That's a good pig," Jeremy said happily, reaching through the fence to scratch Willy behind the ear.

"Looks like you two have become fast friends," Mrs. Ewing remarked.

"Don't get too attached to him, Jeremy," Mr. Ewing warned. "If everything goes as planned, Willy will only be living here long enough to learn how to be a seeing-eye pig. After that he'll go to live with a blind person."

Jeremy knew his father was right. Still, he couldn't bear to think that someday he would have to give Willy away. "Willy's different from the other pigs, Daddy," he said. "He's smaller and weaker. Besides, he likes me. Last night when the two of us were in bed . . ."

"What?" Mrs. Ewing broke in. "Did you take Willy to bed with you?"

Jeremy nodded guiltily. "I wanted to take him somewhere that Rambo couldn't push him around. I put him back into the pen this morning before you woke up."

Mr. Ewing shook his head. 'That's not a good idea, Jeremy. Willy has to learn to take care of himself. He'll never make a good seeing-eye pig if he gets spoiled."

"Willy isn't spoiled," Jeremy protested.

"Let's find out," Mr. Ewing said. He opened the pamphlet and glanced over the first few pages. "We're going to test the pigs' reactions to strangers, to new situations, and to danger," he explained. "The ones that do the best will be the ones we train."

Mr. Ewing reached over the fence and picked up Willy. He took the piglet into the front yard and put him down beside Jeremy's bed. "If Willy comes when I call him," Mr. Ewing continued, "that will show us he knows how to pay attention." He walked to the other side of the bed and stopped. "Willy," he called, clapping his hands, "come here! Come here, boy!"

Willy was rolling on his back in the cool grass. When he heard Mr. Ewing's voice, he hopped to his feet. But instead of running to Mr. Ewing, he ran straight to Jeremy.

Dwight laughed. "Nice try, Willy."

Mr. Ewing picked up Willy and carried him back to the center of the lawn. Immediately, the little pig began rooting in the grass around Mr. Ewing's feet. Then he noticed the Velcro straps on Mr. Ewing's sneakers. He grabbed one with his mouth and pulled. It came open with a loud rip.

"Willy, stop that," Mr. Ewing said. But the piglet was having fun. He ran to the other shoe and opened that strap, too.

While Mr. Ewing was crouched down, closing the straps on his sneakers, Willy stuck his snout into Mr. Ewing's pants pocket and discovered a pack of gum. He took a quick sniff and then pulled it out with his teeth.

"Willy," Mr. Ewing said sternly, "no!"

Too late. Willy had the entire pack of gum in his mouth—wrappers and all—and was chewing noisily.

Jeremy ran over and tried to grab Willy, but the piglet thought it was a game. With a playful squeal, he wiggled away and scampered into the driveway. At the same time, Jeremy heard a loud buzzing noise. He looked up just in time to see Charlie Bruder riding up the driveway on a dirt bike, stirring up a huge cloud of dust.

"Oh, no!" Jeremy cried, running toward the driveway. "He's heading right for Willy!"

"Charlie!" Dwight shouted, straining to be heard over the growl of the motorcycle engine. "Watch out for the pig!"

But Willy had already sensed danger. Seconds before Charlie even saw the piglet, Willy veered off to the left

48

of the driveway. He ran toward the Ewings' trailer—and plowed right into a garbage can! The can fell over with a loud crash, just missing the little pig by inches.

Charlie slammed on the brakes and threw down his dirt bike. Together with the Ewings, he ran over to Willy. "What happened?" he asked anxiously. "Is he hurt?"

Willy was lying on his side with his eyes closed. The pack of gum he was chewing had fallen from his mouth. Hesitantly, Jeremy reached out to touch him. At that moment, Willy opened his eyes and hopped to his feet. With his snout twitching, he ran into the overturned garbage can and began gnawing through a plastic garbage bag in search of food.

"Guess he's okay," Jody said with a laugh.

"Hurray!" Jeremy cheered. He pulled Willy out of the garbage can and gave him a hug.

Mr. Ewing scratched his head thoughtfully. "I don't understand it," he said with a frown. "If Willy was smart enough to avoid getting hit by Charlie's motorcycle, why wasn't he able to steer clear of the garbage can?"

"Your pig probably didn't see my bike at all," Charlie said. "He heard the engine and the noise scared him. That's why he ran away."

"What do you mean?" Mr. Ewing asked uncertainly. "The bike was coming straight at him. He must have seen it."

"Pigs don't have very good eyesight," Charlie explained.

Mr. Ewing looked stunned. "Do you mean to tell me I'm training seeing-eye pigs that are practically blind themselves?"

49

"Talk about the blind leading the blind," Mrs. Ewing muttered, shaking her head.

"It's not that bad," Charlie said, chuckling. "They can see well enough to get around. Plus, they have good hearing and a terrific sense of smell. And they use their snouts the way we use our fingers—to touch and explore things."

Mr. Ewing stared off into space. His forehead was lined with three deep thinking wrinkles. Then slowly, a look of determination came into his eyes. "Well, I'm not about to give up on this scheme yet," he said firmly. "If the pigs' eyesight is weak, we'll simply work on developing their other senses to make up for it."

"I just hope they're smart enough to be trained," Mrs. Ewing said. "So far I haven't seen one of those pigs do anything that would make me think so."

"Oh, they're plenty smart," Charlie told her. "But don't worry," he added with a knowing smile, "I doubt you'll ever be able to make money selling seeing-eye pigs." He glanced at Dwight and winked.

Mr. and Mrs. Ewing looked confused. For a moment, Dwight was, too. Why would Charlie think his family didn't want to make money? Then suddenly, he remembered what he had told Charlie yesterday in Elsie's Cafe. *My father made millions in the stock market. He just bought this farm as a tax write-off.*

"How about showing me your dirt bike, Charlie?" Dwight asked quickly. Before Charlie could answer, Dwight grabbed his arm and practically dragged him over to the dirt bike.

"Hey, what's the big idea?" Charlie demanded, pulling away.

"What was that crack about not making money on

50

the seeing-eye pigs? I thought I told you not to mention anything about us being rich.''

''Yeah, I know,'' Charlie admitted. ''But I figured as long as I didn't tell anyone outside your family it wouldn't matter.''

''Well, it *does* matter. My dad will kill me if he finds out I lied—I mean, if he finds out I told anyone. He wants us to live like ordinary people while we're here. Understand?''

''Okay, okay. Hey, what are all those beds and dressers doing on your front lawn?'' Charlie asked, leaning over to pick up his bike.

Dwight shrugged with embarrassment. How could he explain that his family preferred sleeping under the open sky to fixing the roof of their house? Charlie already thought the Ewings were a little odd. This would surely convince him it was true. ''Oh, they're just there until we rebuild the roof,'' he muttered. ''Just a day or two at the most.'' Then, to change the subject, he said, ''Did I tell you we moved here from Baltimore? We . . . uh . . . we had a big mansion overlooking the Chesapeake Bay.''

''Really?'' Charlie gasped. ''Wow!''

Dwight felt a little guilty about telling such a bald-faced lie, but when he saw the impressed look in Charlie's eyes, he couldn't help feeling pleased.

''Listen, I was wondering if you wanted to go for a ride on my dirt bike with me sometime,'' Charlie said. ''I mean, it's probably nothing compared to the stuff you had back in Baltimore, but still . . .''

''Oh, yeah,'' Dwight lied, ''I had a couple of dirt bikes, and a dune buggy, too.'' Actually, Dwight had never been on a dirt bike in his life and he was dying to try it. He ran his hand over the handlebars and said

51

casually, "Still, I wouldn't mind going for a ride after we get done testing the pigs."

"Testing the pigs?" Charlie asked curiously. "Testing them for what?"

"To see if they'll make good seeing-eye pigs."

Charlie shook his head. "That's a crazy scheme your dad thought up. Pigs are smart, but they're stubborn, too. And they love to get into mischief."

"How do you know so much about pigs?" Dwight asked.

"I learned in 4-H. Last year we did a project where we raised animals to show at the county fair. I raised pigs. One of them won a first-prize ribbon, too."

"Do you still have them?"

"Nope. When the fair ended, I sold them to a meat company in Kansas City. My parents made me put half the money in the bank. With the other half, I bought this." He proudly patted the seat of his dirt bike.

Dwight was impressed. Charlie not only understood pigs, he understood business, too. Suddenly, going to a 4-H meeting sounded kind of interesting. Sure, the kids were bound to be hicks. But if he could learn a thing or two about pork production it might help him with his investments in pork belly futures. *Come to think of it,* he told himself, *I might even be able to convince the kids to let me invest some of their money— for a small commission, of course.*

"Why don't you stick around and help us test the pigs?" Dwight suggested.

Charlie looked pleased. "Sure," he said with a smile. "Then after lunch we can take a ride on the dirt bike. There's an abandoned quarry about a mile from here where we can really rip!"

* * *

Dwight, Charlie, and the rest of the Ewings spent most of the morning testing the pigs. First, they tried teaching the piglets to sit, fetch a tennis ball, and come when called. Of course, Mr. Ewing didn't expect the pigs to be able to do any of those things right away. What really mattered, he explained, was to find pigs that were interested, alert, and eager to please.

Next, the family tested the piglets' reactions to strangers (they used Charlie for that), loud noises, and large objects. During one test, Mr. Ewing slowly rolled a wheelbarrow toward each pig. An aggressive pig, he explained, would attack the wheelbarrow. A scared pig would cower. But a smart pig would calmly move out of the way.

Finally, the Ewings put a collar and leash on each of the pigs and took them for a walk around the yard. They led the piglets up and down the stairs to the porch, around the beds and dressers on the lawn, and through the barn. Mr. Ewing watched closely to see which pigs walked comfortably on the leash, which ones noticed the things around them, and which ones moved carefully on uneven ground.

When all the pigs had been tested, Charlie and the Ewings gathered around the pigpen. Jeremy waited anxiously for his father to speak. *What if Daddy picks Willy to be a seeing-eye pig?* he thought miserably. He tried to imagine what it would feel like to give away his pig to a stranger. The thought made his stomach feel like Mishmash Pudding after it's been put through the blender.

"Okay, pig lovers," Mr. Ewing said. "I've added up all the test scores. There are only three pigs that passed with flying colors, and those are the ones we're going to train."

53

Mr. Ewing opened the gate to the pigpen and walked inside. The pigs crowded around him, snorting eagerly. Jeremy held his breath. "Here they are," Mr. Ewing announced. "The world's first seeing-eye pigs." He leaned over and picked up three piglets—the skinny one with long ears, a fat one with brown spots on its back and a curly tail, and a third one with a short, stubby tail.

Jeremy let out a huge sigh of relief. Willy wasn't going to be trained as a seeing-eye pig. And that meant Jeremy would never have to give him away!

"What about the others?" Dwight asked. "What are we going to do with them?"

"I haven't given it much thought," Mr. Ewing replied. "If the first three pigs train easily, maybe we'll give the rest of them a try."

"Or if that doesn't work out, we could sell them as pets," Mrs. Ewing suggested.

"No!" Jeremy cried. "I want them to be *our* pets—especially Willy!"

"Well, we're not going to decide right now," Mrs. Ewing said. She wiped her hands on her jeans and turned toward the house. "Anybody interested in some peanut butter and Marshmallow Fluff sandwiches?"

The rest of the family went inside to make the sandwiches, but Jeremy stayed behind. He was much too upset to eat. He didn't want Willy to be given away or sold. He wanted the piglet to be his pet, forever and ever.

Jeremy leaned against the pigpen fence and watched Willy. As usual, Rambo was chasing the little piglet and nipping at his tail. *Poor Willy,* Jeremy thought. *He needs someone to take care of him. Someone who loves him, like me.*

Then suddenly, Jeremy had an idea. He took Willy out of the pen and carried him into one of the stalls. He made a soft bed out of straw and laid Willy in it. Then he sat down beside him.

"Mom and Dad want to sell you to somebody else," Jeremy said, scratching the piglet behind the ear. "Either that, or turn you into a seeing-eye pig. But I've got a plan. I'm going to feed you and take care of you and show you how to do special tricks. And I'm going to teach you to do them for me and only me. Then Mom and Dad will have to let me keep you. What do you think about that?"

Willy answered by scrambling into Jeremy's lap, knocking off his glasses, and happily licking his face.

Chapter Seven

The next day, the Ewing family began training the three special pigs. At first, everyone called them Long Ears, Freckles, and No Tail. But Jody wasn't satisfied with that. She thought they needed real names, like Willy and Rambo. But what should they be? She wasn't sure.

The answer came that afternoon while Mr. Ewing, Mrs. Ewing, and Dwight were training the pigs to heel. The piglets were supposed to walk on the left of the humans and slightly ahead, just the way a guide dog does. Whenever one of the pigs slowed down or ran forward, the Ewings jerked lightly on the leash and said "Heel!" in a firm but friendly voice.

Mr. Ewing, Mrs. Ewing, and Dwight were walking the pigs in front of the house when Jody strolled out the front door eating a peanut butter and banana sandwich. Long Ears stopped and sniffed the air. "Heel!" Dwight said.

But Long Ears was too excited by the smell of peanut butter and bananas to obey. Grunting with pleasure, he

56

waddled up the porch steps toward Jody. "Hey!" Dwight cried. "Get back here!" He tugged on Long Ears's leash, but the little pig pulled so hard that he jerked the leash out of Dwight's hand.

When No Tail saw Long Ears running up the steps, he chased after him. "Heel!" Mrs. Ewing said firmly. No Tail was less stubborn than Long Ears. He stopped in his tracks and looked around. "That's right," Mrs. Ewing said. "Come on back here." No Tail started back down the steps.

Freckles was bringing up the rear. His nose twitched as he smelled the peanut butter, but Mr. Ewing held his leash taut and said "Heel" in a reassuring voice.

Unfortunately, at that moment Long Ears leaped up on Jody and pressed his wet snout against her bare knees. "Yuck!' she exclaimed. She reached down to push him off and accidentally dropped her sandwich.

Instantly, Long Ears leaped on the sandwich and began munching away. When the other two piglets saw that, they couldn't control themselves. No Tail took off so fast that the leash flew out of Mrs. Ewing's hand. Freckles got excited and ran between Mr. Ewing's legs, throwing him off balance. He fell to the ground as Freckles followed the other piglets up the stairs.

"Stop it, you three!" Jody ordered. She knelt down to grab her sandwich away from Long Ears, but the little pig knocked her hand away with his snout.

Soon No Tail was beside him. He tried to bite a corner of the sandwich, but Long Ears let out an angry grunt and pushed No Tail aside with his hefty shoulder.

Freckles joined in. He bit No Tail's tiny tail and squirmed up next to Long Ears to grab a piece of the sandwich. Long Ears responded by bonking snouts with No Tail.

"Look at them," Dwight moaned. "It's like a scene out of the Three Stooges."

"That's it!" Jody cried. "We'll call them Moe, Larry, and Curly. Long Ears is Moe because he's the toughest. No Tail is Larry, and Freckles is Curly because he's got the curliest tail."

"I don't care what you call them," Mr. Ewing said, scrambling to his feet and chasing after the pigs. "Just get the little monsters back in their pen!"

By the time the family had separated the pigs, the peanut butter and banana sandwich was in gooey pieces all over the porch. The piglets' faces were smeared with peanut butter, and they had pieces of banana in their ears. As for the Ewings, their hands were sticky and their clothes were splattered with food.

"It's hard to imagine these pigs are ever going to be well-trained enough to live in a house," Dwight said as he carried Moe back to the pigpen.

"Especially if they go berserk every time they get near people food," Jody agreed.

"I certainly wouldn't let them in *our* house," Mrs. Ewing said, wiping a smudge of peanut butter off her chin. "They aren't even housebroken."

"What do you think, Dad?" Dwight asked.

But Mr. Ewing didn't answer. He was standing next to the pigpen with Larry in his arms, gazing off into the cloudless sky. He had peanut butter on his hands and mashed banana on his glasses, but he didn't seem to notice. Then slowly, his eyebrows lifted and his eyes focused. He looked at his family and smiled. "Say hello to our new housemates," he announced. "Moe, Larry, and Curly."

"Housemates!' Mrs. Ewing gasped. "What are you talking about?"

"If we want these pigs to be able to live with blind people someday, we have to get them out of the pigpen and teach them how to live with humans."

"But Dad, they'll destroy our house," Dwight argued.

"It won't be any worse than having a puppy."

"*Three* puppies," Mrs. Ewing corrected.

"Okay, three puppies." Mr. Ewing frowned thoughtfully. When he spoke again, his voice had dropped to a husky whisper. "Training these pigs isn't a game. It's a serious responsibility." He gazed down at the piglet in his arms. "Someday a blind person is going to take this pig into his home. He's going to eat with Larry at his feet, sleep with Larry beside his bed, walk with Larry across busy streets. In short, he's going to trust this pig with his very life."

Jody felt a tingle run down her spine. Up until now, training the piglets had seemed more like an exciting adventure than a serious responsibility. But now she knew her father was right. If they were ever going to turn Moe, Larry, and Curly into seeing-eye pigs, they had to teach them how to live with humans. And that meant training them to live in a house.

Jody looked at her mother to see how she felt about it. "We're going to have to get the roof fixed," Mrs. Ewing said simply. "And bring the beds into the house."

"I'll put a notice up at Elsie's Cafe saying we're looking for a handyman," Mr. Ewing said. He put Larry in the pigpen and wiped his sticky hands on his jeans. "Who wants to drive into town with me—and maybe eat some of Elsie's fried chicken while we're at it?"

"Me!" everyone shouted at once.

* * *

The next day the hot weather broke and a cool breeze wafted through the Ewings' yard, bending the stalks of the sunflowers and rustling the leaves in the trees. After breakfast, Mrs. Ewing drove downtown to attend a meeting of the Yellow Bluff Fourth of July Parade Committee. Dwight left soon after her. He planned to spend the day with Charlie, helping him change the oil in his dirt bike and then going for a ride at the quarry.

After he left, Mr. Ewing, Jody, and Jeremy did the dishes and then went out to the front lawn to put the pigs through their paces. "When are Moe, Larry, and Curly moving into the house?" Jeremy asked.

"Probably tomorrow," Mr. Ewing replied. "I need to buy some diapers first."

"We're going to put diapers on them?" Jody giggled.

"They're just babies. We can't expect too much of them right away."

Jeremy wished he could bring Willy into the house, too. But he knew what his father would say: "Willy belongs in the pigpen with the other outside pigs."

But just wait, Jeremy thought, *someday Willy will live in the house, too—as my pet.*

Just then, a sleek red pickup truck rumbled up the driveway and stopped in front of the house. A middle-aged man in slacks and a yellow polo shirt got out on the driver's side. Then the passenger door opened and an elderly man in faded denim overalls, a work shirt, and sunglasses stepped out.

"Morning, folks," the man in the yellow shirt called. "My name is Ned Glenn, and this is my father, Luther Glenn."

"Good morning," Mr. Ewing replied, walking forward to meet them.

60

"Call me Luther," Luther said loudly, thrusting out his hand in Mr. Ewing's direction. Mr. Ewing took it and Luther gave him a long, vigorous handshake. "I hear you got some notion about training seeing-eye pigs."

"Dad . . ." Ned Glenn said in a warning tone.

Luther ignored him. "Good idea," he said. "Darn good idea. Folks don't realize that pigs is smart. Real smart. Why, one time a pig saved my life."

"Dad, please!" Ned Glenn interrupted.

Luther laughed. "Oh, my son don't understand pigs. He raises them, sure. But he don't understand them. You can't raise happy pigs by stickin' them in stainless-steel cages and pumpin' them full of vitamins. Nope, you gotta treat them right. A happy pig is a tasty pig, I always say."

While Luther was talking, Moe, Larry, and Curly trotted up and began sniffing his shoes. "Hiya, fellers," Luther said. He knelt down and scratched the piglets on the stomach. They rolled over and sighed blissfully.

"The reason we're here is because we read the sign you put up in Elsie's Cafe," Ned Glenn explained. "You see, my father wants to apply for the job."

"I know what you're thinkin'," Luther said, getting to his feet. "I'm too old to be up on a roof hammerin' boards. Well, you're wrong. I still do practically all the work over at our place. Got to, or my son'll hire some city boy who don't know a hammer from a hacksaw."

Mr. Ewing smiled. "Let me show you around the place and tell you what we need, Luther. Kids," he added, "you stay here and look after Moe, Larry, and Curly."

Mr. Ewing and Luther headed across the front lawn and went into the house. Ned Glenn watched them go,

61

then turned to Jody and Jeremy. "I don't mean to be nosy, but why do you have bedroom furniture in your front lawn?"

"Well, we can't sleep in the bedrooms, can we?" Jody said with a shrug. "They're full of broken plaster and stuff."

Mr. Glenn laughed and shook his head. "I have a feeling you folks are going to get along with my dad just fine." He folded his arms over his chest and added, "Frankly, I'd be happy if your father would give him a job and get him out of my hair. He's got nothing to do at home except follow me around, giving advice and getting in the way."

"It sounds like he knows a lot about pigs," Jody remarked.

"He's been a pig farmer all his life. But things have changed. Raising pigs is big business now. You can't succeed by treating the animals as if they were your friends. He doesn't understand that."

"But our pigs *are* our friends," Jeremy said.

Mr. Glenn didn't answer. "Dad's a hard worker though," he said thoughtfully. "I'll give him that." He glanced at Jody. "I mean, you'd figure an old blind man wouldn't be able to do much. But he wears me out just watching him sometimes."

Jody was sure she'd misunderstood. "Did you say . . . blind?"

"You mean he can't see?" Jeremy asked, instinctively reaching up to touch his glasses.

Mr. Glenn laughed. "You couldn't tell? He gets around pretty well, I guess. I've tried to convince him to use a cane, but he won't hear of it."

At that moment, Luther and Mr. Ewing came out of the house. Jody and Jeremy watched as Luther walked

62

down the front stairs. He held his head high and moved with confidence, barely bothering to touch the banister with his hand.

"Well, we're all set," Mr. Ewing said as they walked up. "Luther's going to start on the roof tomorrow."

"Glad to hear it," Mr. Glenn said. Moe, Larry, and Curly were sniffing his socks, but he pushed them away with his foot. "Now, come on, Dad," he said impatiently. "We've got a lot of things to do this morning." He reached out to take his father's arm, but Luther jerked away and walked proudly to the truck by himself.

When Mr. Glenn and Luther were gone, Jody turned to her father. "Did you notice anything . . . uh . . . unusual about Luther?"

"Well, he's an opinionated old guy," Mr. Ewing answered with a smile. "I guess the only thing really unusual about him is that he doesn't think my seeing-eye pig scheme is crazy. Oh, yes, and there was one other thing. He never took off his sunglasses, even when we went into the house."

Jody grinned. "There's a reason for that," she said. "Luther is blind."

Mr. Ewing's mouth fell open. "Blind? But . . . are you sure?"

"Mr. Glenn told us so," Jeremy said with a nod.

Mr. Ewing shook his head and laughed. "Incredible." He thought for a moment and then said, "You know, if we're lucky Luther will end up doing a lot more around here than fixing our roof."

"Like what?" Jody asked eagerly.

Mr. Ewing smiled. "Can you think of anyone better qualified to help us train seeing-eye pigs?"

Chapter Eight

"Rise and shine, lazybones! You can't run a pig farm by lyin' around in bed all day!"

Jody was certain she must be dreaming. She opened one eye and squinted into the dim early-morning light. Luther was standing at the edge of the front lawn wearing overalls and a wide-brimmed straw hat. Mist was rising off the grass all around him, making him look like a ghost out of a Stephen King movie.

In the next bed, Mrs. Ewing began to stir. "What time is it?" she croaked, slowly propping herself up onto one elbow.

"Six o'clock," Luther said loudly. "The sun's up, and you should be, too. The early bird catches the worm, you know."

"I don't like worms for breakfast," Jeremy said in a small, sleepy voice.

Luther laughed loudly. "All right, young feller, then I've got an even better reason for you to get up." He lifted his nose and sniffed the air. "Smell that? Storm's coming. If we don't get that roof replaced in the next few days, you're gonna wake up one morning and discover there's a river runnin' through the middle of your house."

That was enough to get Mr. Ewing moving. "The front door is open," he said as he slipped on his glasses. "Go on in and get started." He motioned toward the piles of planks, boxes of nails, and stacks of roofing tiles that were lined up in front of the house. "I went into town yesterday afternoon and bought everything you told me you'd need."

"Glad to hear it. And have you got some brooms and shovels?"

"What for?" Mr. Ewing asked.

"While I'm workin' on the roof, I want the rest of you to start cleanin' up the fallen boards and plaster on the second floor. My son's bringin' over a Dumpster. You can just shovel everything out the window into that."

"Can I help you work on the roof, Luther?" Jody asked. It wasn't that she wanted to get out of helping to clean up the junk; actually, heaving pieces of plaster out the window sounded kind of fun. But crawling around on the roof sounded even more exciting.

Luther took off his hat and ran a hand through his sparse white hair. "If your ma and pa give the okay, you're welcome on the roof. I'd enjoy the company."

"Can I, Mom?" Jody pleaded. "Come on, Dad. Say yes."

"Well, if Luther thinks it's not too dangerous . . ." Mr. Ewing began.

"No more than climbin' a tree," Luther replied. "And I've got a hunch this young lady has tried her hand at that a few times. Now get up, will ya? The pigs are hungry and I'll bet you are, too."

65

A half an hour later, Mr. Glenn delivered the Dumpster and helped Luther set up a chain hoist to lift the planks and shingles up to the roof. As soon as he left, the Ewings went up to the second floor and started shoveling. While they worked, Luther and Jody opened the ladder and leaned it against the side of the house.

"You go first," Luther said. "Hold on tight and don't look down. I'll be right behind you in case you lose your balance."

"But how could you tell?" Jody asked. "I mean, you can't . . ."

"Can't see?" Luther finished. "That's true. But I can hear you. Besides, if you started to fall, I'd feel the air movin' against my face and know something was wrong."

"You can feel something that gentle?" Jody asked with amazement.

"If I was close enough. When you can't see, your other senses get more sensitive to make up for it."

"That's what Charlie Bruder said about the pigs. Their eyesight isn't that good, but they make up for it with their hearing, their sense of smell, and their snouts."

"And their brains," Luther said, tapping the side of his head with his index finger. "Now climb up there and let's get to work. Time's a-wastin'."

Jody stepped onto the first rung of the ladder and started climbing. Luther was three rungs behind her. They climbed past the first floor, past the second floor (where Jody stopped to wave through the window at the rest of the family), and up to the roof.

"Oooh, I feel like a bird!" she exclaimed. She held onto one of the remaining roof rafters and looked around. The farms of Yellow Bluff were spread out all around her like an endless patchwork quilt. The newly plowed fields were brown, the wheat fields were yellow, and the vegetable fields were green. Buildings looked like the miniature houses in a Monopoly game, and the roads seemed to be pieces of string that stretched out to the horizon. "I've never been up this high before," she said breathlessly. "I can see all the way to downtown Yellow Bluff."

"Look west from the center of town," Luther said. "Do you see a yellow barn next to a little red house?"

"Uh . . . oh, yes, I see it."

"That's my farm," Luther said proudly. "Bought the land in 1946, right after the war."

"Was your son a baby then?"

"Sure was. And my wife was a beautiful bride. She died in 1985. We were married for forty years." While he talked, Luther took a coil of rope out of his pocket. He tied one end around Jody's waist and the other around one of the remaining rafters. "That ought to keep you from doin' any serious damage to yourself. Now climb up on the edge of the house and tell me if the ceiling joists are still in place."

"What's a joist?" Jody asked.

"The planks of wood that frame the ceiling. They're usually two inches thick and six inches wide. Just like the ones your daddy bought at the lumberyard yesterday."

Jody climbed onto the house and looked around. A grid of two-by-sixes covered the second floor of the house. Looking down between them, she could see the ceilings of the upstairs bedrooms and bathroom. The ceilings had gaping holes in them, and through the holes she had a clear view of her family shoveling up broken

67

boards and plaster inside the house. "The ceilings are a mess," Jody told Luther, "but the joists are still there."

"Good. That means we can start layin' the rafters." Luther turned the chain hoist and brought up the first load of two-by-sixes. He lifted one of the planks onto the top of the house and climbed up after it. With Jody's help, he laid it into place against the ridgepole. Then he pulled his hammer out of the loop on the side of his overalls and began hammering the two-by-six down.

Jody watched as Luther worked. First, he ran his hand up and down the board to feel where he wanted the nail to go. Then, without a moment's hesitation, he placed the nail against the wood and started hammering. It slid into place with just two or three firm swings. "How can you do that?" Jody asked.

"Do what?"

"Hammer without being able to see what you're doing."

"Practice. Here, you wanna try it?"

Luther showed her where to put the next nail. Jody held it in place and tapped it lightly with the hammer. Nothing happened, so she swung harder. The hammer hit the edge of the nail, slid off, and smacked her finger. "Ouch!" she cried.

"Try it again," Luther said. "Go slow and concentrate on makin' the head of the hammer hit the nail straight and true."

Jody sucked on her lower lip to help her concentrate. She raised the hammer and took aim. Once, twice, three times she made contact with the nail. Three more tries and the head of the nail was flush with the wood.

"Good job," Luther said as he felt the wood. "Now try another one."

"Luther," Jody asked as she worked, "were you born blind?"

"Nope. I lost my sight in 1942. It was during World War II and I was workin' in a factory in Salina where they made jeeps. I was on the assembly line teachin' a new feller how to install suspension springs. You see, they got a machine there that compresses the spring. Then we was supposed to pick it up with a sort of clamp and put it on the A-frame."

"Was it hard?" Jody asked.

"Not if you paid attention. But this feller was young, and more interested in the girls on the line than in his job." Luther frowned, remembering. "Well, I showed him how to do it a couple of times. Then I gave the clamp to him."

"What happened then?"

"He didn't get a good enough grip on the spring. It uncoiled right into my face. Broke my nose and put out my eyes."

"Oh!" Jody gasped. "That's horrible!"

Luther pushed back his hat and wiped his forehead with his sleeve. "Well, that's life, I guess. You gotta take the bad with the good."

"But weren't you sad?"

"Sure I was. At first. But I got used to it. Now bein' blind just seems natural to me. Of course, that don't mean I can't use a little help once in a while." He reached out and patted Jody's shoulder. "Hey, what are them bumps?" Luther asked with surprise.

Jody looked down. She was wearing one of the shirts her mother had designed. It had bottle tops, Styrofoam packing chips, and paper clips sewn all over it. "It's a shirt my mom made for me," she explained.

69

Luther nodded thoughtfully. "I like it. Now how about nailin' this next board into place?"

Jody grinned happily. "Sure."

Luther rested the two-by-six against the ridgepole and pointed out where the nail should go. Jody steadied the nail and held the hammer above it. Then with one . . . two . . . three firm strokes, she sent the nail sliding into the wood, straight and true.

At noon, everyone stopped for lunch. Mr. and Mrs. Ewing made grilled cheese sandwiches and Suzy Qs fries, and Luther made up a big batch of hand-squeezed lemonade.

"Well, I guess this is as good a time as any to introduce Moe, Larry, and Curly to the house," Mr. Ewing said as everyone carried the food into the dining room.

"But we're just about to start eating," Dwight protested. "When the pigs smell the food, they'll go nuts."

"They've got to get used to that," Mr. Ewing replied. "What do you say, Luther? Do you mind?"

"Mind?" Luther laughed. "I've spent most of my life around pigs. And unlike my son, I like 'em."

"Did you ever have a pig for a pet?" Jeremy asked after Mr. Ewing went out to get the pigs.

"Sure did. Of course, I was raisin' my pigs to sell for meat, so I tried not get too attached to them. But every once in a while a pig came along that was so friendly and so clever, I just sort of fell in love. Old Beth was like that."

"Who's old Beth?" Jeremy asked.

"The best pig I ever had. One night back in '52 my barn caught fire. I was fast asleep and didn't have a clue. Old Beth opened the latch of her stall with her nose, jumped through an open window into my house, and marched right into the bedroom to wake me up. Thanks to her, the barn was saved."

"Wow!" Jeremy exclaimed.

Just then, Mr. Ewing opened the front door and Moe, Larry, and Curly came waddling into the house. Each of the piglets had a collar around his neck, and each was wearing a disposable diaper.

Mrs. Ewing and the children took one look at the pigs and burst out laughing. "What's so funny?" Luther asked.

"They're wearing diapers!" Jody giggled.

Luther chuckled. "Good idea. But you won't need them for long. Pigs are naturally clean. Once they get the idea that this is their home, they'll *want* to go outside to do their business."

By now Moe, Larry, and Curly had smelled the food. Squealing eagerly, they ran into the dining room. "Sit!" Mr. Ewing called, hurrying after them. "Heel!" But they were too busy trying to hop up into his empty chair to listen.

"Get down!" Mrs. Ewing ordered. She leaped to her feet and sat in Mr. Ewing's chair so the piglets couldn't jump on it. Instantly, the pigs changed direction and ran to her chair. Moe and Curly managed to jump on it, but before Curly could get near Mrs. Ewing's plate, Moe shoved him onto the floor.

"Stop it!" Dwight shouted. He reached across the table to whisk his mother's plate away, but instead he accidentally hit his glass of lemonade. It tipped over and poured into Jody's lap.

"Yuck!" she shrieked. "Thanks a lot, Dwight!"

"Forget the lemonade," Mr. Ewing cried. "Get the pigs!"

But before anyone else could make a move, Luther

took over. He grabbed Moe by the collar and carried him into the corner of the room. "This one's the leader," he explained. "If you can control him, you can control them all."

"But what about Larry and Curly?" Dwight asked. The two piglets were still trying to jump into Mrs. Ewing's chair.

"Soo-ie," Luther called softly. "Here, piggies. Soo-ie, pig!"

Larry and Curly stopped jumping. Their ears perked up and they turned toward Luther.

"Soo-ie," he called again.

The pigs trotted over to him. Luther took hold of their collars and sat them down. "Good pigs," he said soothingly, rubbing their ears. "Good boys." Immediately, the piglets began to calm down.

"How did you do that?" Mrs. Ewing asked.

"I've spent a lot of years around pigs and I've learned how to talk to them. If you act calm, they'll calm down. If you get all worked up, they will, too."

"Luther," Mrs. Ewing asked with concern, "do you really think we can turn these piglets into seeing-eye pigs?"

Jody leaned forward, waiting for Luther to speak. If anyone knew the answer, he did. But what if he said no? Then that would mean the people of Yellow Bluff were right—Mr. Ewing was a kook and his idea was just plain silly. *No,* she screamed silently. *It can't be true.* Still, her muscles tensed and her stomach did flip-flops as she waited for Luther's answer.

"Folks," Luther said seriously, "I *know* you can train these pigs. But I think you'd get faster results if you had a real pig expert workin' with you. And maybe someone who was blind, too."

72

"Luther, you're a pig expert *and* you're blind," Jeremy pointed out.

"Well, so I am." Luther chuckled. "Whaddaya know?"

"Would you help us?" Mr. Ewing asked. "We couldn't pay you much, but—"

"I'm not interested in money. All I ask is for Mrs. Ewing to make me a shirt like the one Jody's wearin'. And maybe a few other pieces of clothing, if you've got the time."

"I'd be happy to," Mrs. Ewing said with surprise. "But why—"

"Being blind, I can't see what I'm wearin'. But I can feel it. I'd get a kick out of a shirt like that, and I'll bet a lot of other blind folks would, too. Whaddaya say?"

"It's a deal," Mrs. Ewing said. The rest of the family let out a cheer. Even Moe, Larry, and Curly looked happy. They wagged their curly tails and oinked for joy.

Chapter Nine

"Well, whaddaya think, folks?" Luther asked.

Three days had passed since Luther and Jody began working on the roof. Now, at last, it was finished. The Ewings leaned their heads back and gazed up at the top of the house. The new slate shingles gleamed in the sun. "It's beautiful!" Mr. Ewing exclaimed.

"And not a minute too soon," Dwight said, pointing toward the black rain clouds that were rolling across the sky.

"Come on," Mrs. Ewing said, "let's get the beds inside."

"Better move the pigs out of the pen, too," Luther pointed out. "You don't want 'em catchin' cold."

"We'll bring Moe, Larry, and Curly into the house," Mr. Ewing said. "The rest of them can be put into their stalls."

"I'll do it," Jeremy said, hurrying toward the pigpen.

Ever since Mr. Ewing had selected Moe, Larry, and Curly to be the first three seeing-eye pigs, he'd had less and less time to spend with the other piglets. That meant someone else had to feed them and care for them. More often than not, that someone was Jeremy. He liked to volunteer because it gave him an excuse to spend more time with Willy.

Now, as the sky turned gray and the wind began to howl, Jeremy climbed into the pigpen and put leashes on Moe, Larry, and Curly. After leading them into the house, he hurried back to the pen and ushered the other seven piglets into their stalls. Quickly, he checked to make sure they all had plenty of food and water. Then he went into Willy's stall and sat down in the warm straw.

Willy waddled over and snuggled up beside him. "You hungry?" Jeremy asked. Willy grunted eagerly. Jeremy pulled some raisins out of his pocket and fed them one by one to the little pig.

Since Willy wasn't allowed to live in the house with Moe, Larry, and Curly, Jeremy had decided to turn the stall into Willy's own private house. Last week he had made a bed for the piglet out of a piece of foam and some old blankets. Next, he brought in some of his favorite stuffed animals. Yesterday he had added an old, beat-up milking stool he found in the barn.

"Look what I brought today," Jeremy told Willy. "Pictures to hang on the walls."

He reached under his shirt and pulled out some photographs he had cut from old magazines. There was a picture of a chocolate cake, a drawing of a horse, and a photo of a pig splashing around in a swimming pool. Jeremy took some thumbtacks out of his pocket and nailed the pictures to the wall of the stall.

As he pressed the last thumbtack into the wood, the rain began. It pattered against the roof and turned the dusty pigpen into a mud puddle. "Guess I'm stuck here with you until the rain stops," Jeremy said with a shrug. He turned to Willy and clapped his hands. "Ready for school?" he asked. The little pig jumped to his feet, squealing happily.

Every day Jeremy watched his father teach tricks to Moe, Larry, and Curly. Then Jeremy turned around and taught the same tricks to Willy. So far the little pig had learned to sit, to fetch, and to heel. Later, Jeremy planned to teach him special tricks that even Moe, Larry, and Curly didn't know.

Jeremy grabbed his raggedy old teddy bear from the corner of Willy's bed and tossed it across the stall. "Okay, Willy, fetch!" he ordered.

Willy trotted across the stall, grabbed the teddy bear in his mouth, and brought it back to Jeremy.

"Good boy!" Jeremy exclaimed. He reached in his pocket and rewarded Willy with a candy mint.

When Willy had run through all his tricks, Jeremy sat down on the milking stool and smiled. Things were turning out just the way he had planned. When Willy was with the other pigs, no one thought he was anything special. He never came when Jody or Dwight called him, and he was constantly getting into mischief. But when Jeremy and Willy were alone, it was a different story.

Jeremy gave his piglet a hug. "Everybody thinks you're too naughty to learn anything," he whispered into Willy's soft, pink ear. "But just wait. When Mom and Dad see how good you are around me, they'll have to let me keep you."

"I hear you got pigs living in your house now," Mr. Bruder said as he drove Dwight, Jody, and Charlie to the Sunday night 4-H Club meeting. "Luther Glenn was talking about it down at Elsie's yesterday."

Jody nodded. "Luther says he's never seen pigs fit into a household so fast. They don't even need to wear diapers anymore. When they want to go out, they just stand at the door and squeal."

"You don't say." Mr. Bruder chuckled. "And they don't give you any trouble, huh?"

Jody shrugged. "Not much. Probably the hardest thing is teaching them not to root up the grass carpet."

"Grass carpet?" Charlie repeated incredulously. "You've got grass growing in your house?"

"Sure," Jody replied. "It used to be in the motor home, but we moved it inside."

Dwight could feel his cheeks turning red. Charlie had never been inside his house and he wanted to keep it that way. Otherwise he'd be forced to explain why his multimillionaire family sat on homemade furniture and ate a stew made out of leftovers every Friday night. "So what do you do at 4-H?" he asked, eager to change the subject.

"Lots of stuff," Charlie replied. "Once some pilots from a crop-dusting company in Salina gave a talk. And last month Rob Torres gave a slide show about visiting his grandparents' farm in Mexico."

"What's happening tonight?" Jody asked.

"Tonight is demonstration night. Kids are going to talk about the projects they're working on this summer. Then we'll probably have refreshments and dance. Mr. Van Huff—that's our advisor—lets us bring in tapes from home and play them on his cassette deck."

Mr. Bruder stopped the truck in front of the Yellow Bluff Grange and the kids got out. "Hey, Rob," Char-

77

lie called as a silver pickup truck pulled up behind them. "Look who I brought with me."

"Hi," Rob said, hopping out of the truck. He was a skinny twelve-year-old with straight black hair and tanned skin. "You're Dwight and Jody, right?"

"How do you know our names?" Jody asked.

"Everybody knows about you," Rob replied. He turned to Dwight. "What kind of dirt bike did you have back in Baltimore?"

"Dirt bike?" Jody asked blankly.

Dwight felt his stomach do a backflip. Charlie was the only person he had lied to about owning a dirt bike. That meant Charlie must have told Rob. Dwight swallowed hard. How many other kids had Charlie told? he wondered nervously.

"What dirt bike?" Jody repeated.

"Nothing," Dwight said quickly. "I'll explain later." He hurried up the steps to the Grange. "I think the meeting's about to start."

Inside, there were fifteen boys and girls sitting on folding chairs. They all looked up with interest when Dwight and Jody walked in. But before Dwight could meet any of them, Mr. Van Huff clapped his hands and announced, "Let's get started."

"The meeting will come to order," a girl in a University of Kansas sweatshirt said. "Charlie, would you like to read the minutes from last month's meeting?"

After Charlie read the minutes and the treasurer read his report, the other club members stood up to talk about their summer projects. A girl with yellow pigtails was the first to speak. "One of our female Duroc pigs had babies this spring and I'm raising the litter," she said. "I'm feeding them 17-percent-protein feed, plus additional milled feed to raise them to market

78

weight. At nine weeks they were vaccinated for erysipelas and . . ."

The more Dwight listened, the more impressed he was. This girl really knew a lot about raising pigs. She took it seriously, too. She didn't let her pigs run around her house the way his family did, and she didn't feed them table scraps, either.

Dwight sighed. Why couldn't his family be more sensible? Training seeing-eye pigs was okay if that's what his father wanted to do, but he needed only Moe, Larry, and Curly for that. The other seven pigs were sitting out in the pigpen doing absolutely nothing. Why not fatten them up and sell them to a butcher? Of course they were only mini-pigs and probably wouldn't be worth a lot. Still, anything would be more than they were earning now.

When the talks ended, Dwight joined Charlie and Rob at the refreshment table. It was Lefty Day in the Ewing household, so he reached for a chocolate brownie with his left hand. He was just about to pop it into his mouth when Jody grabbed his arm and pulled him away from the table.

"Hey, what's wrong?" he asked. "I'm using my left hand."

"It's not that," Jody said. "I need to talk to you. Alone."

Dwight followed her into the corner. "What's up?"

"You know that girl with the blonde braids—the one who's raising pigs this summer? She just asked me what it's like to live in a mansion."

"A mansion?" Dwight repeated, trying to sound like he didn't know what she was talking about.

"Yeah. I told her I didn't live in one, but she said

she was talking about when we lived in Baltimore. She said you told Charlie we're rich.''

"Rich?" Dwight laughed nervously. "Why would I say something like that?"

"That's what I want to know. And what was all that talk about dirt bikes? You never owned a dirt bike in your life."

"Well, uh . . ."

Jody snatched the brownie from his hand. "Come on, Dwight. Confess."

"Oh, okay," Dwight admitted, "I did tell Charlie we're rich. I said Dad brought us here so we could see how regular people live."

"But why?"

"So Charlie wouldn't think we're a bunch of loony tunes—which we are."

"We are not!" Jody cried indignantly.

"Oh, come on. Do you know any other family with a father who invents grass carpets and a mother who sews bottle caps on shirts?"

"Well . . ."

"And how many typical American families have three pigs running around their house? Face it, Jody. We're weird."

"Well, so what?" Jody demanded. "I don't want to be normal. It's boring."

"But it's embarrassing." Dwight shrugged. "I mean, it was okay when I was a kid. But now I'm thirteen years old—a teenager!"

"Well, I don't care," Jody said. "I'm not going to go around telling everybody we're rich. It's a lie. Besides, what if Mom and Dad find out?"

Dwight didn't want to think about that. "You won't tell them, will you?" Jody didn't answer. "Come on," he pleaded, "I'll do all your chores for a week. Or maybe I could invest some money for you. Low risk, high yield. You're practically guaranteed to make money."

Jody shook her head. "There's only one thing that will stop me from squealing. You have to promise to tell the kids the truth—we're not rich and we never have been."

"But Jody, they'll think I'm a total dweeb."

"You should have thought of that before you shot off your mouth, Mr. Moneybags." With that, Jody popped Dwight's brownie into her mouth and walked away.

"Hey, what was all that about?" Charlie asked, walking up.

"Nothing important." Dwight turned to him. "Look, I thought I told you to keep your mouth shut about my family being rich."

"I'm sorry," Charlie said sheepishly. "It just kind of slipped out. I mean, it's not every day a celebrity moves into Yellow Bluff."

"I'm not a celebrity!"

"Well, almost. Listen, some of the guys are going to the swimming hole for a moonlight swim. You wanna come? It's at the bottom of the field behind the Grange."

Dwight shrugged. He was mad at Charlie, but a moonlight swim sounded like a real adventure. Besides, it would give him a chance to get Charlie alone and tell him the truth about the Ewings. "Okay," he said.

Dwight found Jody with some of the other girls, eating brownies and listening to the music. He told her where he was going and then went outside with Charlie, Rob, and a boy with freckles and shaggy brown hair.

"You're Dwight, right?" the boy asked as they

81

walked through the field behind the Grange. "I'm Billy. Hey, is it true you had a maid to clean your room back in Baltimore?"

Oh, no! Dwight thought. Rob wasn't the only kid Charlie had blabbed to. Dwight ran his hand through his wavy hair and tried to think. He knew he should tell the truth before things went any further. But how could he? If the guys found out he'd lied about being rich, they'd never let him live it down.

"Sure he did," Charlie answered for him. "They had a cook, too. And when he moves back I'm going to go visit him. Aren't I, Dwight?"

Charlie looked so pleased and proud that Dwight couldn't bear to disappoint him. "Sure," he said. "You can all come."

"All *right*!" Billy exclaimed.

The boys walked through the tall grass until they came to a creek. They followed it until it widened into a deep pool ringed with willow trees. Charlie, Rob, and Billy threw off their clothes and did noisy cannonball dives into the water. Dwight followed. It was a hot night and the water felt cool against his skin.

"You must be really bored living here in Yellow Bluff," Rob said as they splashed around. "I mean, don't you miss living in a mansion with maids and butlers and all?"

Dwight thought about his promise to Jody. He knew he should come clean right now before things went any further. But all the guys were looking at him, waiting eagerly to hear what he was going to say. It made him feel important, and that was a feeling he was learning to like. "Sure I miss it. But Dad says he might sell our mansion in Baltimore and build one right here."

"Here?" Billy gasped. "In Yellow Bluff?"

82

Dwight nodded. "Dad's thinking of getting into pork production. He wants to buy some of the pig farms in the area and start a little operation ourselves. You know, just 50,000 pigs or so."

"But that's all the pigs in Yellow Bluff," Charlie said anxiously. "And if you bought our farms, we'd have to move away."

"No, you could stay and work for us," Dwight replied. He climbed out of the swimming hole and gazed down at the boys like a king surveying his kingdom. He wasn't thinking about his promise to Jody now. All he was thinking about was showing off. "You know," he said grandly, "I never did like the name Yellow Bluff. What would you think of Ewingville instead?"

Chapter Ten

Dwight was sitting on the pigpen fence, drinking lemonade and reading the *Wall Street Journal*. His glass was only half empty but the sun was so hot that the ice cubes had already melted. He took a sip of the lukewarm liquid and watched the piglets rolling in the cool mud. How he wished he could jump into the pen and join them!

Dwight opened the newspaper to the commodities page. Last night at the swimming hole he had convinced Charlie, Rob, and Billy to give him ten dollars apiece to invest in pork bellies. Dwight glanced down the page and frowned. Pork bellies were dropping. He wondered if he should invest his friends' money in something else. But then he'd have to admit he'd been wrong, and he didn't want to do that—especially not after the way he'd bragged that he knew the commodities market like the back of his hand.

Mrs. Ewing walked out of the barn with a bag of feed in her arms. "Here you go, guys," she said, emptying the bag into the pig trough. "Lunchtime."

Snorting with excitement, the piglets waddled over to the trough and began gulping down the food.

"They sure can eat," Dwight said.

"You're telling me! Every one of these pigs goes through three pounds of feed a day. That's twenty-one pounds for all seven of them. One hundred and forty-seven pounds a week!"

"Those pigs should be making money for us," Dwight said, "not the other way around. Anyway, I thought you were going to sell them for pets."

Mrs. Ewing nodded. "We were. But your father and I have been too busy to even think about it. Maybe next month." She watched Willy work his way up to the trough. "I'm going to hate to see them go. They're awfully cute."

"Cute?" Dwight said dubiously, watching the pigs slobber over their food. "That isn't the first word that comes to my mind."

Mrs. Ewing chuckled and wiped her hands on her blue jeans. "Speaking of pig feed, we're almost out. How would you like to go downtown with me and buy some?"

"Sure. Charlie told me that Elsie just installed a video game in the cafe. I want to try it out."

"I'll give you a ride to Elsie's Cafe if you come to the farm store first and help me carry the pig feed to the car."

Dwight closed the newspaper and hopped down from the fence. "It's a deal. Just let me get my money."

As Dwight ran to the house, Jody walked by with Curly. She was wearing a scarf over her eyes so she'd be forced to rely on the piglet to lead her. "Did you do what you promised?" she asked, grabbing Dwight's

85

arm. "Did you tell Charlie and the other kids we're not rich?"

Dwight was glad Jody was blindfolded so she couldn't see the guilty look on his face. "Well . . ." he began.

Jody frowned. "If you didn't keep your promise," she warned, "I'm telling Mom and Dad."

"I said I'd tell the kids and I did," Dwight lied.

"Good," Jody said happily. She dropped his arm and let Curly lead her up the porch steps.

Dwight hung behind. He felt trapped. If his parents found out he'd lied about being rich, they'd be furious. If his friends found out, they'd hate his guts. Dwight remembered one of his grandfather's favorite sayings. "As good old Willy Shakespeare put it," Grandpa Ewing liked to say, "what a tangled web we weave when first we practice to deceive."

Dwight sighed. At the rate he was going, he'd probably tie himself in knots before long.

A half an hour later, Dwight and Mrs. Ewing walked into Baum's Farm Supply. The tiny store was crowded with tools, farm equipment, and bags of feed and fertilizer. Dwight stopped at the gumball machine at the front door. His mother walked ahead and joined the people at the counter who were placing orders.

While Dwight was putting his penny in the machine, a heavyset man with bulldog jowls and thinning hair walked in the door.

"Well, this is a surprise, Mr. Reilly," one of the sales clerks said, stepping up to shake the man's hand. "You usually don't show your face around these parts until September."

"Something new is happening in Topeka this year,"

Mr. Reilly said. "We got people ordering 100-pound roaster pigs and smaller. Some kind of new gourmet delicacy, I suppose. I don't ask questions. If people come into my butcher stores wanting little pigs, I'm going to give them little pigs."

"Can't argue with the public," the clerk agreed.

"Nobody around here wants to sell to me though. They say they can get a better price if they let their hogs grow to full size. If you hear of anyone willing to sell immature pigs, let me know. The smaller the better."

When Dwight heard that, he forgot all about gumballs. If this man was looking for small pigs, he realized, his family might be able to sell the seven surplus pigs right now. It would be a lot easier than selling them one by one for pets, and Mr. Reilly would probably pay more money, too. Dwight hurried toward the counter, eager to tell his mother what he'd heard.

Then suddenly, an incredible idea popped into his head. Why not sell the pigs himself? His parents were always trying to get him interested in the farm. Just think how happy they'd be if he found a way to take the seven extra pigs off their hands *and* bring in some good money at the same time!

Dwight rushed back to where the men were talking. "Excuse me, Mr. Reilly," he began. "I couldn't help overhearing what you said. I have seven mini-pigs for sale if you're interested."

Mr. Reilly's eyes widened. "You bet I'm interested. Are they healthy?"

"Yes, sir."

"How much do they weigh?"

"I'm not sure. They're not full-grown yet, but they're gaining weight every day."

"Well, I'll stop by and see them. If they look good, I'll pay you fifty dollars a pig. What do you think about that?"

Wow! Dwight thought happily. But he knew a good businessman wasn't supposed to look too eager, so he shrugged and said, "I might be interested."

"When can I see them?" Mr. Reilly asked.

Dwight thought fast. His family was going into town after dinner to see a movie. Maybe he could pretend he was sick and stay home. "How about seven o'clock this evening?"

"It's a deal," Mr. Reilly said with a shake of his bulldog jowls.

Dwight grinned. In a few hours he was going to get rid of seven worthless pigs and make $350. He could hardly wait to see the expression on his parents' faces when he handed over the money. Dwight shook Mr. Reilly's hand and gave him directions to the farm. Then he strolled to the counter to join his mother.

Dwight was in the bathroom, practicing looking sick in front of the mirror. Curly was at his feet, stretched out on the cool tile floor.

"The Ewing Express is leaving in exactly two minutes," Mr. Ewing called from downstairs. "All aboard!"

Dwight fixed an unhealthy expression on his face and walked downstairs. Curly followed and joined Moe and Larry on the grass carpet. "Dad, I don't feel so good," Dwight said weakly. "Maybe I'd better not go to the movie."

"Dwight Ewing is giving up a chance to go into town and have some fun?" Jody exclaimed. "Oh, no, he must be dying!"

Jeremy giggled, but Mrs. Ewing hurried in from the

88

kitchen with a worried look on her face and asked, "What's wrong, hon?"

Dwight didn't like to lie, especially when his mother looked so concerned. *But it's for a good cause,* he reminded himself. "My stomach feels yucky," he said.

"Try some Tummy Tamer," Mr. Ewing suggested. Tummy Tamer was a recipe Mr. Ewing had invented to settle upset stomachs. It consisted of chocolate ice cream, bicarbonate of soda, and flat Coke, all mixed together in the blender. It tasted delicious and it worked, too.

"Maybe I should stay here and make you some," Mrs. Ewing suggested.

"Oh, no," Dwight said quickly. "You go ahead and enjoy the movie. I'll be okay. Really."

"But this was going to be the first time we left Moe, Larry, and Curly alone," Jody reminded them.

Shut up, Jody! Dwight wanted to scream. Instead, he turned to the pigs and said, "Larry, stop that!"

"What did he do?" Jeremy asked.

Actually, the piglet hadn't done a thing, but it was 6:45 and Dwight was getting desperate. "He was rooting in the carpet," he lied. "See, it's a good thing I'm staying home. I don't think they're ready to be left alone yet."

"Maybe you're right," Mr. Ewing said. "Well, take care of yourself, son. We'll be back around 9:30."

Dwight watched with growing excitement as his family got in the station wagon and drove away. As soon as they were out of sight he went out to the pigpen and brushed off the seven piglets with a stiff brush so they'd look their best. He was hard at work when Mr. Reilly drove up in a black pickup truck loaded with wire cages.

"Evening, son," he said as he got out. "You ready to make a deal?"

"You bet," Dwight answered, motioning toward the pigpen. "Well, what do you think?"

Mr. Reilly looked them over. "Hmmm, not bad. Normally, I'd pass on that little one," he added, pointing to Willy, "but this year I think I can use him." He nodded, shaking his jowls. "Yep, I'll take them. Fifty dollars per pig."

"Sixty," Dwight said.

Mr. Reilly frowned. "Wait a minute. I thought we agreed on fifty."

"You said fifty, but I didn't agree." Dwight tried to look relaxed and cool, as if he made deals like this every day. "I heard what you said in the farm store. We're the only folks around that are willing to sell immature pigs. So that makes them worth sixty dollars apiece."

"You drive a hard bargain, son." He ran his hand over his thinning hair, thinking it over. Then he thrust out his hand and said, "Boy, you got a deal."

Dwight shook hands. He tried to keep a straight face, but the corners of his mouth kept creeping up to his cheeks. Finally, he just gave in and grinned.

"Okay, son, help me load them up." Mr. Reilly opened the back of his truck and pulled out seven cages.

Dwight climbed into the pigpen. The pigs ran up to him, grunting happily, and he leaned down to pick up Rambo. But then the piglet caught sight of the cages. Squealing with fear, he leaped out of Dwight's arms and scurried into the far corner of the pen. The other pigs followed him and soon all seven were huddled in the corner, grunting fearfully.

90

"I think they remember the last time they were in a cage," Dwight said. "They didn't like it much."

"Hogwash!" Mr. Reilly huffed. "Pigs can't remember further back than their last meal. Now, come on, load them up. I've got to get down to the train station before the stationmaster goes home."

"They're going to Topeka on the train?" Dwight asked.

"Yep. They'll be on the 6:45 out of Yellow Bluff tomorrow morning, but I'm driving back to Topeka tonight—and I'd like to get there before midnight, if you don't mind."

"Okay, sure." Dwight dragged each of the pigs, kicking and squealing, out of the corner of the pen and put them in the cages. The last one was Willy. Unlike the other pigs, he didn't struggle. He just lay limply in Dwight's arms and whimpered.

Dwight and Mr. Reilly loaded the cages onto the truck. Then Dwight signed a bill of sale and Mr. Reilly handed him a check for $420. As Mr. Reilly drove slowly up the driveway, Dwight could see the piglets staring at him with large, sorrowful eyes. A lump rose in his throat and he had to turn away.

Dwight sighed. He felt rotten and he couldn't figure out why. All he'd done was sell some useless pigs to a butcher. That was what pork production was all about—raising pigs to sell for meat. *So why do I feel like a murderer?* he wondered.

He glanced down at the check in his hand. "Four hundred and twenty dollars," he said out loud. Just saying the words made him feel better. He thought about how happy his parents were going to be when he showed it to them. Maybe they'd be so grateful they'd give part of the money to him. Not a lot, mind you.

Just enough to buy himself a secondhand dirt bike, kind of like the one Charlie had.

Dwight smiled. He felt better—much better. With dreams of growling engines and squealing tires zooming through his head, he walked past the empty pigpen and went into the house.

Chapter Eleven

Jeremy woke up the next morning just as the sky was beginning to turn light. With a yawn, he threw off the covers and got out of bed. He could hear the soft snoring of his parents in the master bedroom, and the deep, rumbling snores of Moe, Larry, and Curly sleeping beneath their bed. With his sneakers in his hand, he tiptoed past their door and down the stairs.

Although no one in the family knew it, Jeremy had been getting up at sunrise every morning for the last week to play with Willy. It was their special time together, a chance for Willy to run in the fields behind the house, and an opportunity for Jeremy to teach him new tricks. In fact, sometimes it was their only time together because during the rest of the day Jeremy was busy helping his family train Moe, Larry, and Curly.

Jeremy opened the front door and walked into the yard. Usually the piglets left their stalls and waddled into the pigpen as soon as they heard his footsteps. But this morning the pen was empty and still.

That's weird, Jeremy thought with a frown. He

opened the door that led to the stalls and walked inside. "Willy," he called, "wake up, you lazy pig!"

Silence. Jeremy felt his stomach tighten. He hurried to Willy's stall and looked inside. Empty! He ran down the length of the stalls. Every one of the seven pigs was gone!

Tears welled up in Jeremy's eyes. He turned and ran frantically back to the house. "Mommy! Daddy!" he sobbed as he staggered in the door. "Willy's gone!"

Dwight appeared at the top of the stairs wearing his pajama bottoms and a T-shirt. "Shhh!" he whispered. "That's supposed to be a secret until after breakfast."

"Wha . . . what do you mean?" Jeremy stammered.

"Come outside," Dwight said. "And be quiet." He tiptoed down the stairs and led Jeremy out to the porch. "Mom said the extra pigs cost too much to feed, so I sold them. I got over $400, too."

"You sold Willy?" Jeremy gasped in disbelief.

"I sold them all. See, I overheard this guy talking in Baum's yesterday—"

"You can't sell Willy!" Jeremy cried. "He's mine!"

"Yours? What are you talking about? The pigs belong to the whole family."

"Hey, what's going on out here? It's practically the middle of the night."

Jeremy and Dwight turned to find Jody standing in the doorway, rubbing her eyes.

"Dwight sold Willy!" Jeremy wailed. "He sold all the pigs except Moe, Larry, and Curly."

"Sold them?" Jody cried, turning to stare at her big brother. "Dwight, have you lost your mind?"

Dwight frowned. "Lighten up, will you? Someone's got to use some business sense around here. Those pigs were just taking up space. They would have eaten us

94

out of house and home if I hadn't cut a deal with a Topeka butcher.''

"You sold them to a butcher?" Jody cried in horror. "That's the same as murdering them!"

"Murder?" Jeremy gulped. "You mean they're going to kill Willy?" He began to cry even louder.

"Hey, what's the big deal with Willy?" Dwight asked defensively. "I can't tell one pig from the other."

"But he's my pet," Jeremy said, sniffling. "I take him for a walk every morning, and feed him mints. I even decorated his house." He grabbed Jody and Dwight's hand and led them into the pig stalls. "See? And I'm teaching him tricks, too. I'm going to show Mom and Dad and then they'll see that I have to keep Willy."

Dwight stared at the furniture and pictures that decorated Willy's stall. He looked stunned. "But . . . but why didn't you tell anybody?"

"It was going to be a surprise. Besides, everyone's too busy with Moe, Larry, and Curly to care about Willy. But I care about him." He broke down and sobbed pitifully. "I love him!"

"Jeremy, don't cry," Jody said helplessly. "We'll get Willy back. We'll get them all back, I promise."

Jeremy rubbed his eyes with the back of his hand. "How?" he gulped.

"I . . . I'm not sure." She turned to Dwight. "Where are the pigs now?"

"At the train station, I guess. Mr. Reilly said he's shipping them to Topeka on the 6:45 train."

Jody thought a moment. Then her eyes lit up. "Dwight, can you borrow Charlie's dirt bike?"

"Sure. He said I can use it anytime I want. He even told me where he keeps the keys."

"Well, go get it. We're going to the train station."

"The train station?" Dwight shook his head. "I don't know, Jody. I mean, those pigs are sold. We can't just—"

"Dwight, we have to," Jody said seriously. "For Jeremy's sake."

Dwight looked down at his little brother's tearstained face. "Well . . . okay," he said reluctantly. "But you guys are too young to ride the dirt bike. Besides, it only seats two."

"Then its up to you," Jody said. "Go to the station and get those pigs. We'll follow on my bike."

Dwight turned and ran down the driveway toward the Bruder farm. As soon as he was out of sight, Jody and Jeremy hurried into the house. Quickly and quietly, they changed their clothes and left a note for their parents. Then they went to the barn and wheeled Jody's bicycle into the yard. Jeremy climbed onto the seat. Jody got in front of him and pedaled standing up while he held onto her waist.

At first the bike wobbled so wildly it almost fell over. But by the time they reached the end of the driveway, Jody was pedaling straight and true. She turned onto the road and took off in the direction of downtown Yellow Bluff.

Any other time, Jeremy would have been thrilled to be riding with Jody on her bike. But today he barely felt the breeze in his hair or noticed the fields of wheat flashing by. He was too busy worrying about Willy. He closed his eyes and mouthed the same words over and over: "Please let him be okay. Please, please, please!"

Dwight was on Charlie's dirt bike, roaring down Yellow Bluff Highway. As he rode, he tried to make sense

96

of what had happened. *I don't get it,* he thought defensively. *All I was trying to do was help my family make some money for a change. That's why I sold the pigs.* But instead of being grateful, Jody and Jeremy were mad at him. It just wasn't fair.

But then Dwight remembered Jeremy's tearstained face and his quavering voice. "Everybody's too busy with Moe, Larry, and Curly to care about Willy," he had said. "But I care about him. I love him!" The memory made Dwight's heart ache. *If I had known how much he loved that dopey pig,* he thought guiltily, *I never would have sold him.*

But maybe it wasn't too late. Maybe there was still a chance to get Willy back. But he had to hurry. With new conviction, he opened the throttle and headed for town at top speed.

Fortunately, downtown Yellow Bluff was still asleep. The sidewalks were deserted and there wasn't a car in sight. Still, Dwight forced himself to slow to a crawl as he entered downtown. The dirt bike was meant for off-road riding only. If a policeman stopped him, he'd have a lot of explaining to do.

Dwight coasted down Main Street and turned the corner at the Prairie Savings and Loan. The time-and-temperature clock was just changing from 6:43 to 6:44. Only one minute until the train was scheduled to leave! Dwight's heart thudded against his chest. He opened the throttle of the dirt bike and tore down the last block to the station. He wasn't thinking about the police now. All that mattered was getting there before the train left.

As he rode up to the station, his hopes soared. The train was still there! He threw down the dirt bike and ran to the tracks. The stationmaster and some of the workers were standing outside the station, talking and

97

laughing. Dwight hurried toward them, shouting, "Hold the train! Hold the train!"

The stationmaster turned around. It was Mr. Harrigan, the man with the bushy eyebrows who had been working the day the Ewings first picked up their pigs. "What's wrong?" he asked with alarm.

"There are seven pigs on that train that belong to me. Mr. Reilly brought them here last night. He wants to take them to Topeka, but they can't go."

Mr. Harrigan pulled a clipboard off his belt and flipped through some papers. "The pigs belong to John Reilly," he said. "I've got a copy of the bill of sale right here."

"But it's a mistake," Dwight said impatiently. "I can't sell them to him. I need them back. Hurry, before the train leaves!"

"I'm sorry, son, but I don't have the authority to do that," Mr. Harrigan said. "You'll have to contact Mr. Reilly if you want to call off the sale."

"But he's in Topeka. There isn't time. Please, just let me get my pigs."

The stationmaster crossed his arms over his chest and shook his head. "Can't do it, son. Now go on home. We've got work to do."

"Yeah," one of the workmen added, "and while you're at it, how about putting on some clothes?"

The workers laughed loudly. Dwight gazed down at his baggy T-shirt and pajama bottoms. He'd been in such a hurry to get to the station that he'd forgotten to change. He blushed furiously and turned away.

"Come on, boys," Mr. Harrigan ordered, "let's get to work. We're three minutes behind schedule."

Dwight wandered around the side of the train station. Tears stung the corners of his eyes, making it hard to see where he was walking. *Why did I have to go and sell those pigs?* he wondered miserably. He knew the answer: for money. But somehow the $420 didn't seem so important now.

Dwight let out a ragged sigh. How he dreaded the moment when he would have to tell Jeremy the truth—Willy was on his way to the butcher shop . . . and certain death.

"Dwight! What happened?"

Dwight looked up to see Jody and Jeremy riding up. They hopped off the bike and ran toward him.

Dwight hung his head. "The stationmaster wouldn't give them to me. He said they belong to Mr. Reilly now."

"No!" Jeremy cried. "Willy's mine!"

"If they won't give the pigs to us," Jody said, "then we'll just have to take them."

"But how?" Dwight asked. "The train is about to leave."

"I don't know. We'll think of something. Come on!"

Dwight and Jeremy followed Jody to the platform. Mr. Harrigan and the workers were at the front of the train, talking to the engineer. Suddenly, Dwight had an idea. "Jody, you go and distract the men," he said. "Cry, scream, faint—anything. Just make sure they don't see what we're doing. Jeremy and I will search the freight cars for the pigs."

Jody thought a moment. Then she took off up the tracks in the direction of the workmen, waving her arms and screaming at the top of her lungs, "Help! Help!"

While Jody was yelling, Dwight and Jeremy ran down the tracks, peering into each of the cars and calling, "Willy? Are you in there, Willy?"

The first twenty cars contained nothing but bags of

99

feed and grain. The next ten were filled with cattle. They shuffled their hooves and mooed as Dwight and Jeremy ran by. Then came five cars of chickens, clucking and flapping their wings inside their cages.

Suddenly, a loud burst of air shot out of the brakes of the train. The boys leaped backwards. "What was that?" Jeremy asked fearfully.

"I think the train is getting ready to leave," Dwight answered.

"But Jody—"

"Maybe she couldn't stop them any longer." He peered up the length of the platform, but neither Jody nor the workers were anywhere in sight. "Come on," he told Jeremy, "we've got to hurry!"

The two boys continued running down the track. With each car, Dwight became more and more discouraged. Maybe Mr. Reilly had sent the pigs on an earlier train, he thought. Maybe they were hidden behind some bags of feed or some chicken cages. Or maybe they were in one of the cars at the very front of the train.

Then finally, as Dwight reached the very last car, he heard a faint grunting sound. "Pigs!" he cried, running to the door.

"Willy!" Jeremy shouted. "Willy, are you in there?"

A loud squeal broke through the grunts.

"That's him!" Jeremy exclaimed. "I know it!"

Dwight lifted Jeremy into the freight car and then climbed in himself. The first thing that hit him was the smell. It was disgusting! He held his nose and looked around. The car was packed from front to back with cages, each one containing one or more pigs. The only way to see which pig was in which cage was to climb on top of them and peer inside.

Yuck! Dwight thought with disgust. The smell was

gross enough at the door. He didn't want to get any closer. But Jeremy was already climbing across the cages, calling, "Willy! I'm here, Willy!"

The squealing grew louder. It was coming from a cage in the middle of the car. Jeremy crawled to it and looked inside. "Here he is!" he shouted triumphantly. "I found Willy!"

Dwight was so relieved, he forgot all about the smell and climbed across the cages to join Jeremy. "Okay, you grab that end and I'll grab this end," he instructed. "Now lift!"

Jeremy wasn't very strong, but together they managed to lift the cage over the others and drag it to the door. As Dwight jumped to the platform to carry Willy down, he saw his parents driving up in the station wagon.

"What are you doing here?" he asked in amazement.

"Jody left a note," Mrs. Ewing explained as she and Mr. Ewing hurried across the platform to join the boys. "Did you find Willy?"

"He's in here," Jeremy said, pointing to the cage.

"Thank goodness!" Mr. Ewing exclaimed. "Now, let's find the other pigs."

With their parents' help, Dwight and Jeremy soon found all seven pigs and transferred them from their cages to the car. As they were lifting the last pig from his wire prison, Jody came running down the tracks at top speed.

"Did you find them?" she gasped as she skidded to a halt.

"Yes," Dwight said. "How did you keep Mr. Harrigan from finding us?"

"I told him I was the mayor's cousin," she said with a grin, "and if he didn't hold the train until my uncle got here with a shipment of wheat, he'd be fired. When he finally got suspicious and called the mayor's office, I slipped out of the station and took off.''

"That means any minute he might come looking for you,'' Dwight said anxiously.

"He already has,'' Mrs. Ewing said, pointing toward the station. "Look.''

Mr. Harrigan was striding down the platform with a grim look on his face.

"Let's go, kids,'' Mr. Ewing said, herding them toward the car. "Quick!''

The family jumped in the station wagon and slammed the doors. Mr. Ewing backed out of the parking lot so fast he sent up a spray of dust and gravel. As they drove away, Dwight heard the long, shrill blast of a train whistle. He turned and looked out the back window just in time to see the train slowly chugging out of the station.

Dwight let out a sigh of relief and leaned his head against the back of the seat. The pigs were safe! Suddenly, he felt something wet and scratchy in his ear. With a gasp, he spun around. Jeremy was sitting in the back of the station wagon with Willy in his arms. The little piglet was wagging his tail and grunting happily.

"Did that pig of yours lick my ear?'' Dwight asked, pretending to be grossed out.

"That's Willy's way of saying thanks,'' Jeremy said. "He loves you, Dwight.'' He leaned over the seat and gave his big brother a hug. "And so do I.''

Chapter Twelve

As soon as Willy and the other pigs were back home in their pen, Mr. Ewing took Dwight aside and asked, "Why did you sell those pigs without asking us?"

"I wanted to surprise you," he answered. "I mean, I know we don't have much money, and I figured $420 would come in handy. Besides, you and Mom are always trying to get me interested in the farm . . ."

"What we're trying to get you interested in is work," Mr. Ewing said.

"But I *am* working," Dwight insisted. "I'm helping you train Moe, Larry, and Curly, aren't I? And I'm keeping track of my commodities investments, too."

"Okay, okay. Just promise me there won't be any more sneaking around behind our backs. And no more secrets."

Dwight stared down at his shoes. He still had one secret his father didn't know about. Charlie and the guys still thought his family was rich. Dwight frowned. Ever since the night of the 4-H meeting, he'd been meaning to tell them the truth. But it was so hard! He loved it when the guys asked him questions about being a millionaire. They really looked up to him, and that made him feel important.

Still, he knew that sooner or later he had to tell Charlie the truth. "Okay, Dad," he said. "No more secrets."

"And this afternoon I want you to send Mr. Reilly's check back to him with a letter explaining why you can't sell the pigs, and apologizing for any inconvenience you caused him."

"Are you still going to sell the pigs for pets?" Dwight asked.

"I haven't thought about it. But if anyone sells those pigs it will be your mother and me, not you. Got it?"

"Got it, Dad."

After Mr. Ewing went inside, Dwight walked over to the pigpen. Willy and the six other piglets were waddling around the pen, making happy homecoming noises. When they saw Dwight, they ran over to greet him. "Welcome home, guys," he said. "I'm glad you're back." He was surprised to discover that he really meant it.

The days went by in a steady blur of blue skies, high temperatures, and hard work. The Ewings, with Luther's help, were turning Moe, Larry, and Curly into first-class seeing-eye pigs. By the end of July, the pigs had learned to sit, come when they were called, fetch, walk calmly on a leash, heel, and stay. During meals, they sat quietly under the table. They were completely housebroken and they stayed off the furniture. They didn't even root in the grass carpet anymore.

One Tuesday morning, Jody was in the front yard, watching Luther practice his bike-riding. Luther was training Curly to sit in a basket on the handlebars and alert him whenever the bike veered too far to the left or right.

"Okay, Curly, let's try it again," Luther said, rolling up the sleeves. He was wearing one of the shirts Mrs. Ewing had designed for him. It was made from rough, unbleached cotton and had fat pink pigs embroidered all over it.

Luther clutched the handlebars and pedaled slowly down the driveway. Soon the bike began veering to the right. Jody held her breath. Another few feet and Luther would ride right into a tree!

Suddenly, Curly oinked loudly and moved to the left side of the basket. Luther felt the movement and corrected his mistake by turning the handlebars slightly to the left. The bike straightened out.

Jody grinned. "Good pig, Curly!" she called.

Luther and Curly continued down the driveway. Each time Luther drifted to the left or right, Curly oinked and shifted his weight. When they arrived at the road, Curly grunted twice to let Luther know there was danger ahead. Then they turned around and started back.

When they stopped in front of the house, Jody clapped enthusiastically. "That pig really knows his stuff!" she exclaimed.

"Hey, Jody," Luther said, "I got me an idea. Whaddaya say we take Moe, Larry, and Curly downtown and surprise your folks?"

Mr. Ewing had driven to Baum's Farm Supply to buy a new hose. Mrs. Ewing had gone into town with him. Lately, she'd become interested in local history. Whenever she had a spare hour or two, she went to the library or the town hall and looked through their collections of old photographs, newspapers, and documents.

105

"Downtown?" Jody repeated. "But Moe, Larry, and Curly haven't been off the farm since the day they came here."

"They're gonna have to learn sometime. They'll never be real seeing-eye pigs until they know how to guide us through crowds and traffic."

Jody laughed. "There isn't much of either of those in Yellow Bluff."

"Well, we don't want to take them into downtown Kansas City right off the bat, now do we?" He chuckled. "No, I think Yellow Bluff is just perfect for their first trip into the real world."

Jody grinned, imagining how surprised her parents would be when they saw Moe, Larry, and Curly strolling through downtown Yellow Bluff. "I'll go get the harnesses," she said.

A few minutes later, Luther, Jody, Dwight, and Jeremy met in the front yard. Everyone was filled with nervous excitement. Even the pigs could feel it. They struggled and grunted when Luther put on the special leather harnesses Mrs. Ewing had made for them. And when they realized they were being led down the driveway and into the road, they forgot all about heeling and started to run.

"Hold it right there, fellas," Luther said. He pulled on Curly's leash until the piglet stopped running. Jody did the same to Moe, and Dwight held Larry. Jeremy stood in the street and blocked their way like a traffic cop stopping traffic.

The pigs turned and waddled slowly back to Luther and the children. They knew they'd been bad and they looked embarrassed. Luther knelt down and talked soothingly to them. As usual, his very presence seemed to calm them down. "All right," he said, patting the pigs on their rumps, "now let's try it again."

Luther and the children started down the road. This time Moe, Larry, and Curly stayed at their heels. The first time a car came by, the piglets let out a squeal and cowered in the grass. But Luther calmed them down, and soon they were waddling along like experienced seeing-eye pigs.

As they headed into downtown Yellow Bluff, Jody proudly looked down at Moe. The piglet was walking slowly and confidently beside her. When they came to a curb, he hopped up onto it without a bit of trouble. Jody smiled. She could hardly wait for the people of Yellow Bluff to see Moe, Larry, and Curly. *Then they'll have to admit Daddy was right,* she thought. *Pigs* are *smart enough to be trained.*

Up ahead, two women came out of the Prairie Savings and Loan and strolled toward Luther and the kids. *Oh, boy,* Jody thought eagerly, *they're coming our way.* "Good morning!" she called.

The women took one look at the Ewing children and their pigs and stopped dead. Then they turned in their tracks and hurried off in the opposite direction.

"What's the matter with them?" Dwight asked.

"Maybe they don't like pigs," Jeremy suggested.

The next store they came to was Ed's Barbershop. "I wanna stop in and say howdy to Ed," Luther said. He pushed open the door and called, "Hey, Ed, you in there?"

Ed was cutting a little boy's hair. "Morning, Luther," he said. When he saw Curly, he laughed. "What the heck are you doing with that pig?"

"This is my seeing-eye pig," Luther said. "You know I've been helpin' the Ewings to train them."

"Ewings!" Ed muttered with a sour expression. "Don't mention that name around here." Then he noticed Dwight, Jody, and Jeremy standing on the sidewalk behind Luther. "I'm mighty busy right now, Luther," he said in a chilly voice. "Maybe you'd better come back some other time."

Luther closed the door of the barbershop. "Well, what do you suppose that was all about?"

"Maybe they don't like us walking the pigs in town," Jody said.

Dwight shook his head. "It's not the pigs. Ed didn't start acting funny until he saw *us*."

"Let's see if your daddy is in Baum's," Luther said. "Maybe he knows what's up."

Mr. Ewing was coming out of the farm store when they arrived. "Good heavens!" he gasped when he saw the pigs. Then his face broke into a grin. "Did you walk all the way from the farm?"

"You bet," Luther replied. "The pigs have been good as gold, too. Even trucks don't scare them."

"Daddy, has everyone been acting mean to you today?" Jeremy asked.

Mr. Ewing frowned. "Come to think of it, yes. I keep saying good morning to people, but they don't answer me. And Mr. Baum insisted he didn't have the hose I wanted, even though I saw it hanging on the wall right behind him."

"It's been the same thing with us," Jody said. "You'd think we had the plague or something."

"Let's go find Mom," Dwight said. "Maybe she knows what's going on."

Mr. Ewing nodded. "Good idea. We were planning on having lunch at Elsie's Cafe. We can all go together."

108

"Now you're talkin'," Luther said. "That joint serves up more gossip than fried chicken. If there's a rumor goin' around town, we're sure to hear it there."

They found Mrs. Ewing in the town hall, poring over some old maps. "Yes, now that you mention it, I have noticed that people seem to be avoiding me," she said pensively. "I thought maybe it was the sour cream and onion omelettes we had for breakfast this morning."

Everyone tried to laugh, but it came out like more of a groan. Jody frowned. She was used to her family being thought of as outsiders, even weirdos. But this was different. The townspeople were acting as if the Ewings had done something wrong. But what?

Mr. and Mrs. Ewing, Luther, the kids, and the pigs left the town hall and headed down the street to Elsie's Cafe. Each time they passed someone, Jody met the person's eye and smiled. But the look she received back was a combination of anger, suspicion, and fear. Jody thought it might have made sense if the people had been staring at Moe, Larry, and Curly. After all, most of the citizens of Yellow Bluff thought pigs belonged in a pen, not strolling down the sidewalk. But the expressions on the townsfolks' faces weren't directed at the pigs, or even at Luther. Those angry expressions were meant for the Ewings alone.

Still, Jody's spirits began to lift as she walked through Elsie's parking lot. Elsie would explain what was going on, she told herself. Probably it was just some kind of silly misunderstanding. Jody smiled, pictured herself biting into a piece of crispy fried chicken and laughing at the whole ridiculous mix-up.

Suddenly, Mr. Ewing stopped in his tracks. "Look," he said glumly.

Jody looked. Elsie was peering out the window of

the restaurant. When she saw the Ewings looking back at her, she quickly lowered the curtain and moved away from the window. A second later, a hand appeared and placed a CLOSED sign on the door.

"Hey, they're not closed," Jody protested. "I can see people eating in there."

"What's going on?" Dwight asked indignantly.

"I'm going to go find out," Jody said, taking a step toward Elsie's front door.

But Mr. Ewing grabbed her arm and stopped her. "Don't make a scene, honey. Let's go home and talk to the Bruders. They'll tell us what's going on."

"That's right," Mrs. Ewing said, trying to sound cheerful. "Besides, we've got something better than fried chicken. What do you say we make Mishmash Surprise for lunch today instead of dinner?"

Normally, an announcement like that would have made Jody cheer. But today she could barely manage a smile. Only a half an hour ago, she realized, she had been bursting with happiness, eager to show off Moe, Larry, and Curly to the whole town. Now she felt as if someone had slapped her in the face.

"This town is weird," Dwight muttered as they walked away.

Jody frowned. For the first time since they'd moved to Yellow Bluff, she wondered if maybe Dwight wasn't right.

Chapter Thirteen

"Hey, look," Jeremy announced as they drove up the long, tree-lined driveway to their farm, "someone's waiting for us."

There was a black-and-white police car parked in front of the house. A man in a tan uniform with a silver badge on his shirt pocket was standing beside the car.

"Who is it?" Luther asked.

"A policeman," Dwight told him. "A tall guy with a crew cut and sunglasses."

"That's Dan Peabody," Luther said, "the local sher-iff. He's got the cunning of a fox and the warmth of a hungry rattlesnake."

"What do you suppose he wants with us?" Jody asked.

"I think we're about to find out," Mr. Ewing said. He opened the door and got out. The rest of the family followed. "Good morning, Sheriff," he said with a smile.

"I guess some people might think so," the sheriff said gruffly.

Mr. Ewing stopped smiling. "What's the problem, sir?"

Sheriff Peabody pulled a piece of paper out of his back pocket and handed it to Mr. Ewing. "Just this."

"What is it, Dad?" Dwight asked.

Mr. Ewing pushed his glasses up his nose and read over the paper. "A fine," he said. "For . . ." His eyes widened. ". . . three thousand dollars!"

"There must be some mistake," Mrs. Ewing said. "We didn't do anything wrong."

"I beg to differ, ma'am," the sheriff said. He took the paper from Mr. Ewing and began to read. "Town ordinance number 117: No pigs are allowed within the limits of downtown Yellow Bluff unless said pigs are transported in secure, locked cages."

"But this morning was the first time we ever took our pigs downtown," Mr. Ewing interrupted. "Couldn't you just give us a warning? We promise it won't happen again."

"This morning was not the first time," the sheriff snapped. "You've been spotted transporting pigs in your car without cages on two separate occasions."

"But we couldn't help that," Mrs. Ewing protested. "Our station wagon isn't big enough for ten cages."

"Then there's town ordinance number 121," the sheriff continued. "Any farmer who wishes to raise pigs for slaughter must apply for a permit from the sheriff's office."

"But we aren't raising pigs for slaughter," Dwight argued. "Moe, Larry, and Curly are seeing-eye pigs. The rest are pets."

"That's not what Rodney Harrigan down at the Yellow Bluff train station says. He's got a record of a bill

112

of sale for seven mini-pigs from Dwight Ewing to John Reilly of Reilly's Meat Markets in Topeka.''

"That was a mistake!" Dwight cried. "The pigs are still here. See?" He pointed to the pigpen where Willy and the other piglets were lying.

Sheriff Peabody didn't bother to look. "And last, but certainly not least," he said, "is town ordinance number 132B: No pigs shall be kept inside a dwelling that is primarily intended for human beings."

Dwight's mouth dropped open. Moe, Larry, and Curly weren't allowed in the house? He couldn't believe it. He glanced over at the rest of his family. They looked as dumbfounded as he felt.

"But . . . but . . ." Mr. Ewing stammered, "Moe, Larry, and Curly have been living with us for weeks. Nobody ever told us it was against the law."

"Ignorance of the law is no excuse," the sheriff said flatly.

"Oh, get off your high horse, Peabody," Luther burst out. "The Ewings ain't hurtin' anyone. Their pigs are clean and healthy, and they're housebroken, too. Plus, they're smart and friendly—which is more than I can say for that mangy dog you got runnin' around your property."

"That's enough out of you, old man," Sheriff Peabody growled. "You've always been a little loony. I'm not a bit surprised you'd side with these people over your own neighbors."

"Hey, you can't talk to Luther like that!" Jody cried angrily.

The sheriff ignored her and turned to Mr. Ewing. "You can either pay a $3000 fine or spend thirty days in jail. Let me know what you decide." He shoved the paper into Mr. Ewing's hands. "Good day, Mr. Ewing." With that, he got into his car and drove away.

Dwight stared at the police car as it bumped down the driveway. He felt sick inside and his knees were weak and shaky. "What are we going to do, Dad?" he asked.

Mr. Ewing was staring off into space, the way he often did when he was about to come up with one of his marvelous ideas. For a moment, Dwight's hopes lifted. But then his father let out a heavy sigh and said, "I don't know, son."

Mrs. Ewing smiled sadly. "Well, I guess we know now why the folks downtown were snubbing us."

"You think they knew the sheriff was waiting for us?" Jody asked.

"I can't think what else it could be."

"I don't mean to pry," Luther broke in, "but do you figure you can pay the fine?"

"Just barely," Mr. Ewing answered. "But it will clean us out. We'll have to sell the farm. And the pigs, too."

"Not Willy!" Jeremy cried. "You can't sell him!"

"Jeremy, we're just talking about possibilities," Mrs. Ewing said gently. "Nothing is decided yet."

Jeremy's lower lip began to tremble and he looked as if he was about to burst into tears. He ran to the pigpen and reached through the fence to hug Willy.

Dwight watched sadly. *I saved Willy once,* he thought. *I wish I could do it again.*

Then suddenly, Dwight had a wonderful idea, one that made him feel incredibly noble and generous. He would sell his pork belly futures and give the money to his parents to help pay the fine!

With his heart pounding in anticipation, Dwight ran

114

into the house. Pork bellies had been going up the last few weeks. Last time he looked, his fifty-dollar investment had increased to almost one hundred and fifty. With any luck, it might have gone even higher.

The *Wall Street Journal* was lying on his bed where he'd left it this morning. Dwight opened it to the commodities page and searched impatiently for the livestock section. There it was—pork bellies.

"Oh, no!" Dwight moaned. Pork bellies had taken a huge nosedive. If he sold now he'd only end up with forty-five dollars—five dollars less than he started with. That wasn't even close to what he would need to help his parents save the farm.

Dwight got up and went to the window. He leaned his forehead against the glass and gazed down at the front lawn. When he'd first moved here, he realized, he would hardly have cared if his family had lost the farm. In fact, he probably would have been happy. Back then, he thought Yellow Bluff was a hole in the ground and the people in it were a bunch of hicks.

But over the last month, things had changed. Charlie, Rob, and Billy had become his friends. He was even starting to like Yellow Bluff. He still thought it was too small and too hot. But back in Baltimore he'd never splashed in a swimming hole, ridden a dirt bike through a quarry, and eaten mouth-watering fried chicken at Elsie's Cafe.

And then there were the pigs. They weren't dumb animals to him anymore. Now he thought of them as family pets. He remembered what his father had said after the sheriff left—"We'll have to sell the farm. And the pigs, too." Dwight shook his head. Moe, Larry, and Curly were used to living in a house and eating people food. They'd be miserable on a regular farm.

115

And what about Willy? Dwight looked down at the pigpen. Willy was lying on his side in the dirt, happily basking in the morning sun. *Jeremy will never get over losing him,* Dwight thought. And then he realized something. "Neither will I," he said out loud.

No one slept very well that night. Even Moe, Larry, and Curly seemed to know something was up. Instead of curling up in their usual spot under Mr. and Mrs. Ewing's bed, they roamed through the house, grunting anxiously.

Up in his bedroom, Jeremy was tossing and turning, deep in the throes of a horrible nightmare. In it, a tall, hulking man was rounding up the piglets and tossing them into a truck. Jeremy picked up Willy and tried to run away. But the man grabbed both of them and threw them over his shoulder. "Put me down!" Jeremy cried. "I'm not a pig!"

The man laughed and tossed Jeremy and Willy into the back of the truck with the rest of the pigs. As he climbed into the driver's seat he roared, "You're all going to Mr. Reilly's butcher shop in Topeka, Kansas!"

"No!" Jeremy wailed. He gathered up Willy in his arms and held him close. As they drove away, the little pig reached up and anxiously licked his face.

Jeremy awoke with a start. Something really *was* licking his face!

"Willy!" he gasped, looking down at the little pig lying on the pillow beside him. "How did you get in here?"

Willy only grunted and snuggled a little closer.

"Were you having a bad dream, too?" Jeremy asked. He smiled. Willy must have sneaked out of his stall and climbed in an open window. Jeremy put his arm around

116

his piglet and held him close. "Don't worry," he said. "You're with me now. I won't let anyone hurt you."

Willy let out a contented sigh and closed his eyes. But Jeremy couldn't sleep. The memory of his nightmare was still fresh in his mind. How could he save Willy from the butcher shop if his parents were forced to sell the farm?

Willy was soon fast asleep. But Jeremy lay there a long time, staring into the darkness and worrying about what tomorrow might bring.

Chapter Fourteen

"Wake up, everyone! Wake up!"

Jody opened her eyes. She sat up and tried to figure out if the voice she'd heard had been real or part of her dreams. Before she could decide, her father stuck his head in her room and called, "Family meeting at the pigpen in five minutes." Then he continued on down the hall, shouting, "Wake up, everyone! Wake up!"

Jody threw on her robe and went downstairs. As she trudged across the front lawn, she thought back to the first night her family had come to the farm. How happy she had been sleeping in her bed under the stars! Back then, training seeing-eye pigs had seemed like much more than an exciting adventure. It had been a chance to finally prove to the world that her father wasn't a goofy eccentric—he was a brilliant thinker whose unusual ideas really, truly worked.

Now they'll never know, she thought sadly.

"Why so glum, chum?"

Jody looked up to see her father leaning against the pigpen fence. To her surprise, he was smiling.

"What's there to be happy about?" Jody asked.

"Nothing," Dwight said, walking out of the house to join them. Jeremy and Mrs. Ewing followed, along with Moe, Larry, Curly, and Willy.

"I have to agree," Mrs. Ewing said gently. "Things look pretty grim."

"Oh, I don't know about that," Mr. Ewing said. "We may be down, but we're not out. Not yet, anyway."

"But what about the fine?" Jody asked.

"We'll pay it if we have to," Mr. Ewing said. "But not without a fight." He took a seat on the top rail of the fence and gazed down at his family like a general about to address his troops. "I went to bed last night feeling totally defeated. I was ready to pack up the motor home and leave town this morning. Then I realized I was sick and tired of running away with my tail between my legs. This time I'm going to stay and fight."

"But how, Daddy?" Jeremy asked.

"My first thought was to hire a lawyer. But we don't have the money for that. Then I decided to go to the mayor and talk things over with him. But when I saw the newspaper this morning, I had an even better idea." He pulled the paper out of his robe pocket and opened it. "Take a look," he said, pointing to a column with the headline *Events and Activities Around the County*.

Jody read the first listing. "Yellow Bluff Town Council Meeting. Tonight at 8 P.M. in the Yellow Bluff Grange."

"Are you going?" Dwight asked.

"We all are," Mr. Ewing replied. "And the pigs, too."

"The pigs?" Mrs. Ewing gasped.

Mr. Ewing nodded. "We're going to show the people of Yellow Bluff that Moe, Larry, and Curly are trained seeing-eye pigs, not livestock," he said with determination. "And that we're pig trainers, not criminals."

Jody felt excited, but scared. "Do you think the pigs are ready?" she asked. "I mean, what if they misbehave?"

Mr. Ewing was about to answer when, to everyone's surprise, Luther came strolling up the driveway.

"Luther!" Mrs. Ewing exclaimed. "How did you get here? Where's your son?"

"Nothin' like a brisk walk to get the old blood circulatin'. Besides, I figured the way things are goin', you could use a little moral support this mornin'."

"Luther," Mr. Ewing said, "I want to take Moe, Larry, and Curly to the town meeting tonight and show everyone what they can do. You think they're ready?"

Luther grinned. "Ready as they'll ever be. Anyhow, I'll come along and keep them in line. That is, if it's okay with you."

"Of course," Mr. Ewing said warmly. "I was hoping you'd come."

Luther took off his hat and fanned his face. "Wouldn't miss it for the world. Those town council members need to get knocked on their butts now and then—and this sure as heck oughta do it!"

The Ewings pulled up in front of the Grange at exactly eight o'clock. Luther had spread the word around Yellow Bluff that the family would be there (he didn't mention the pigs), and it looked as if the whole town had shown up. Cars were parked along the road and up on the grass, and there were people spilling out the door of the Grange.

Dwight nervously smoothed down his hair as he got out of the car. He felt anxious and worried. What if the pigs acted up? Or what if his father got one of his famous faraway looks in his eye and gave a speech about how "the brain of the humble pig is inferior only to that of primates and dolphins." Dwight felt sure he'd die of embarrassment.

Mr. Ewing and Dwight went around to the back of the station wagon. Moe, Larry, and Curly pressed their noses to the glass, eager to get out. Behind them, Willy snorted with excitement.

At the last minute before they had left home, Jeremy had insisted that he be allowed to bring Willy, too. Mr. Ewing had finally agreed, on the condition that the little piglet stay in the station wagon during the meeting. Now Jeremy came to the back of the car and asked, "Why can't Willy come in, too, Daddy?"

"Because tonight we want the town council to see our trained pigs. I told you that before."

"But Willy *is* trained," Jeremy insisted. "He can do tricks."

"Yeah," Dwight teased, "like untie shoelaces and steal food off people's plates."

Before Jeremy could answer, someone at the door of the Grange shouted, "Hey, they've got their pigs with them!"

"Take your hogs and clear out of Yellow Bluff!" someone else cried.

Still someone else yelled, "This is our town. We won't sell!"

"What are they talking about?" Mrs. Ewing whispered as the family led Moe, Larry, and Curly inside. "Sell what?"

"I don't know," Mr. Ewing said with a frown.

121

Inside the Grange it was wall-to-wall people. All the folding chairs were filled and there were dozens more people standing in the back. Luther was waiting inside the front door. When he heard the grunts of the pigs, he grinned and came forward to join the Ewings.

The mayor and the four town council members were sitting at the front of the room behind a long table. Mayor Clinton was a tall, lanky man with a thin, weather-beaten face and a shock of dark hair. When he saw the Ewings, he picked up his gavel and pounded the desk. "It is against the law to bring livestock in here," he announced in his booming voice. "Please remove them immediately."

The whole room fell silent. Mr. Ewing stepped forward and said firmly, "These animals are not livestock. They're seeing-eye pigs. They're housebroken, they obey commands, they—"

Henry Bruder jumped to his feet. "Just because your pigs can do a few parlor tricks don't mean you can make us forget why you came to Yellow Bluff."

"Yeah," shouted Ed the barber. "We aren't selling out to you, no matter how rich you are!"

"What are you talking about?" Mr. Ewing asked with a confused frown.

"Don't play innocent with us," a woman cried. "This is Yellow Bluff, not Ewingville—and it's going to stay that way!"

Dwight froze. *Ewingville*. He knew he'd heard that name somewhere before. But where? Then, with a horrible sinking feeling, he remembered. That night at the swimming hole after the 4-H meeting, he had told Charlie and the guys that his family planned to buy up all the farms in the area and rename the town Ewingville.

Dwight's stomach felt like it had just been hit by a

122

typhoon. His cheeks burned and his skin prickled from head to toe. He wanted to run out of the Grange and keep running until Yellow Bluff was just a distant memory. But he knew he had to stay and set things straight. He knew it was time to tell the truth.

"Mayor Clinton," he said in a shaky voice, "I . . . I have something very important to say."

The crowd was still shouting, but the mayor hit the table with his gavel and growled, "Pipe down, everyone!" The room fell silent. Everybody—including the rest of the Ewings—turned to stare at Dwight. "Well, go on, son," the mayor said. "We haven't got all night, you know."

Dwight cleared his throat and looked around the room. "Ever since my family moved here," he began, "people have been laughing at us. They think we're weirdos because we're trying to train seeing-eye pigs. Well, the truth is, I used to think the idea was pretty goofy, too. And I didn't like being laughed at. It was embarrassing.

"Then I met Charlie Bruder. I wanted him to like me, so I lied. I told him my family was rich and my parents only moved to Yellow Bluff to show us kids how ordinary people live. I said we were training seeing-eye pigs so my dad could claim the business as a tax write-off."

"But Dwight," Jody cried with dismay, "you promised me you were going to tell Charlie the truth."

"I know," he said with a guilty sigh. "And I meant to. But I was afraid all the guys would hate me if they found out I'd lied." He shrugged helplessly. "Anyway, one thing led to another and pretty soon I made up some other lies. Like I said my dad wanted to buy up all the farms in town and make one huge pig farm. And I said he was going to change the name of the town from Yellow Bluff to Ewingville.''

Mayor Clinton looked stunned. ''You mean to say you made that up?''

Dwight nodded. ''Yes, sir.''

The mayor turned to Mr. Ewing. ''Is your son telling the truth? Are you rich or aren't you?''

Mr. Ewing laughed ruefully. ''We're not rich. Not even close.''

For a long moment, the mayor didn't say anything. Then he pounded the table with his gavel and demanded, ''Where's Henry Bruder?''

Mr. Bruder stood up. ''Uh, right here, sir.''

''When you came into my office last week, you told me Prairie Savings and Loan was planning to repossess the farms of all the families that were behind on their mortgage payments and sell them to Mr. Ewing.''

''Well . . . uh, I thought it was true.''

''You mean to tell me you believed the silly stories of this young boy?''

''Well . . . no. Not right away. I mean, when my son first told me what Dwight said, I was skeptical. But then I saw Mrs. Ewing at the town hall looking over all the real-estate records for the last fifty years. Now, why would she be doing that if they weren't trying to buy us out?''

''Yeah,'' a voice in the crowd demanded, ''why?''

''Because I'm interested in local history,'' Mrs. Ewing said. ''And it wasn't only the real-estate records I was looking at. I've been looking through all the old maps and documents in the town hall and the library.''

''We never had the slightest intention of buying your farms,'' Mr. Ewing said earnestly. ''We wouldn't have the money to buy them even if we wanted to.''

"And besides, we don't want to," Jody added. "We're not pig farmers. We're here to train seeing-eye pigs."

Mr. Baum from the farm-supply store stood up. "That still doesn't change the fact that you broke the law," he said. "Pigs aren't allowed to live in houses, and that's that."

"You're right," Mr. Ewing conceded. 'We did break the law. We didn't mean to, but we did. But we're here tonight to try and convince you that the laws are unjust. You see, our pigs are not livestock and they shouldn't be treated that way. They're pets. And more than that, they're seeing-eye pigs, specially trained to guide the blind."

"Pigs is pigs!" shouted a chubby man in overalls— the same man who had laughed at the Ewings the first time they went into Elsie's Cafe. "You can't train 'em to do nothing except eat slop and roll in the mud."

"You're wrong," Mr. Ewing said calmly. "And with your permission, Mayor Clinton, we'll prove it."

"Well . . . all right, go ahead," he said sternly. "But make it fast. This is a town meeting, not a live-stock auction."

"Yes, sir!"

Quickly, Mr. and Mrs. Ewing took scarves out of their pockets and blindfolded themselves. Luther held Curly's leash, Mr. Ewing took Moe, and Mrs. Ewing led Larry.

"To guide a blind person," Mr. Ewing began, "the seeing-eye pig must walk on the person's left side, just slightly ahead. If there's an obstacle in the way, the pig must lead the blind person around it."

Mr. and Mrs. Ewing and Luther shook the pigs' leashes. Moe, Larry, and Curly led them slowly up the

125

aisle. When Mr. Ewing said, "Left," the pigs turned left. When he said, "Right," they turned right. When he said "Stop," they stopped in their tracks, and when he said, "Hup-up," they walked faster.

"Now, Jody, will you please come down here and walk toward us?" Mr. Ewing asked.

Jody got up and walked briskly down the aisle. At first it appeared that she was going to walk right into Luther. But then Curly veered to the right and led Luther around her. Moe and Larry did the same. A murmur of surprise and approval ran through the crowd.

Dwight watched from the back of the hall. As the pigs performed, he smiled proudly. And then he realized something. He used to be embarrassed to watch his parents walking with the pigs, but now he wasn't. After all, he told himself, it hadn't been easy to train Moe, Larry, and Curly. Not many people could have done it—or even thought up the idea. But his father had not only dreamed up the scheme, he had seen it through—*and* succeeded!

"Now, watch this," Mr. Ewing told the crowd. "When a blind person drops something, his guide pig must pick it up and bring it to his left side."

Luther took his wallet out of his pocket and tossed it on the floor a few feet in front of him. "Fetch," he said. Curly trotted to the wallet, picked it up, and brought it back to Luther's left side.

"Big deal," the chubby man shouted. "They obey now, but throw those pigs a scrap of food and they'll forget everything you taught them."

"You think so?" Mr. Ewing asked. "Watch." He took a cookie out of his pocket and put it on the floor among the pigs. They sniffed the air and let out an eager snort. "No," Mr. Ewing said firmly. "Sit."

126

Moe, Larry, and Curly sat down. "Now forward," Mr. Ewing said. The pigs led their masters up and down the aisle past the cookie. Not once did they so much as touch it. In fact, they never even looked at it!

The pigs were still performing when Dwight noticed Jeremy slip out the door. "Hey, where are you going?" Dwight whispered. But Jeremy was gone.

A moment later, Dwight heard someone behind him let out a gasp. He spun around in time to see Jeremy walk back into the room. But this time he wasn't alone. He had Willy with him—and the little piglet was walking on his hind legs!

"Well, will you look at that!" someone exclaimed.

Everyone turned to look at Jeremy and Willy.

"Why, I didn't know pigs could do tricks!" exclaimed an elderly lady in rimless glasses.

"And what a cute little boy!" cooed the woman behind her.

But Dwight wasn't amused. What if Willy pulled one of his usual stunts—like knocking off someone's glasses, or getting loose and running around the room? That was all it would take to make the crowd forget the good things Moe, Larry, and Curly had just done.

Dwight looked up at his parents. They had pulled off their blindfolds and were walking toward Jeremy with worried looks on their faces. But before they could get to him, Jeremy faced the crowd and announced, "This is my pet pig, Willy. I'm teaching him tricks. Play dead, Willy."

With a pitiful moan, Willy flopped down on his side and closed his eyes. The whole room burst out laughing. Dwight's jaw dropped. He couldn't believe what he was seeing. Willy was a born show-off. And the crowd seemed to love it.

"Now, roll over, Willy," Jeremy instructed. Willy opened his eyes and rolled over.

"Good boy! Now, dance!"

Willy hopped to his feet. Jeremy began to clap his hands and stamp his foot, like a caller at a square dance. Willy responded by shaking his rear end back and forth and grunting happily.

When the crowd saw that, they burst into applause. Even Mayor Clinton and the town council members joined in.

"That pig is adorable!" the lady with the rimless glasses cried.

"And smart, too," someone else agreed.

Suddenly, Elsie from Elsie's Cafe jumped to her feet and shouted, "I want to make a motion. I propose we repeal town ordinances 117, 121, and 132B. From now on, pet pigs can ride in cars, enter public buildings, *and* live in houses."

Mayor Clinton grabbed his gavel. "All in favor?" he asked. The four members of the town council raised their hands. "Good. It is unanimously passed." He pounded the table. "I think we've had enough excitement for one night. Meeting adjourned!"

As the last word left the mayor's lips, Willy broke away from Jeremy and trotted to the front of the room. With a happy grunt, the piglet leaped into Mayor Clinton's lap and planted a wet kiss on his face. "Yuck!" the mayor cried. The room shrieked with laughter. Mayor Clinton tried to smile as he wiped his face with a handkerchief.

Mr. Ewing rushed to the table and grabbed Willy from the mayor's lap. "Thank you, Mayor Clinton," he said. "And thank you, Yellow Bluff. And now, ev-

128

eryone is invited to Elsie's Cafe. The fried chicken is on us!''

''Hooray!'' the crowd exclaimed, heading eagerly for the door.

Dwight pushed his way through the departing crowd and joined his family as they made their way to the door. ''Mom, Dad,'' he said as they walked outside, ''this whole stupid mess has been my fault. I'm sorry I lied, *really* sorry.''

Mr. Ewing gazed sternly at his son. ''You deserve to be punished, young man, and believe me, you will be.'' Then his face broke into a smile. ''But we'll worry about that later. Right now it's time to celebrate.'' He threw his arm around Dwight's shoulder. ''Let's go to Elsie's and *pig out*!''

Chapter Fifteen

It was the end of August, and Dwight was in the pig stalls, raking out the old straw and replacing it with new, clean hay. As his punishment for lying, his parents had ordered him to take care of the pigs for the rest of the summer—both the house pigs and the ones that lived out in the pigsty. That meant buying their food, feeding them, washing them, mucking out the pen, and cleaning out their stalls.

Dwight paused to wipe the sweat from his brow. It was the hottest day of the summer—105 degrees in the shade, according to the thermometer in the barn. He sniffed the soiled, smelly straw and wrinkled his nose. "I hate pigs!" he muttered.

At that moment, Jeremy and Willy came into the stall. "You don't hate Willy, do you, Dwight?" Jeremy asked with a worried frown.

"No, of course not." He crouched down to scratch Willy behind the ears. "I could never hate *him*." And he meant it. Since the night of the town meeting, the whole family had come to realize that Jeremy and Willy really did have a special bond. The little piglet lived in the house now and, unlike Moe, Larry, and Curly, he was terribly spoiled. "I'm just sick of cleaning out these stalls, that's all."

"Well, you can stop now," Jeremy replied. "It's time to make Mishmash Surprise."

"Huh? This is Thursday, not Friday."

"I know, but I have a sore throat. Mom said Mishmash would make it feel better."

"Sounds good to me." Dwight threw down his rake and followed Jeremy and Willy into the house.

Inside, they found the rest of the family—plus Luther—gathered in the kitchen. "I found some leftover noodles," Jody said, kneeling in front of the refrigerator.

"Toss them in," Mrs. Ewing said. Jody handed the storage bowl to Luther and he emptied it into the stew pot.

Dwight washed his hands and joined his sister at the refrigerator. "Here's some tomato soup," he said, "and some home fries, and a dish of peas and carrots."

When everything had been dumped into the pot, Mrs. Ewing added one cup of beef stock and some spices. She turned on the stove and said, "Mishmash Surprise, coming right up."

A half an hour later, everyone was sitting at the dining room table, mopping up the Mishmash with hunks of bread. Moe, Larry, and Curly lay obediently at their feet. Only Willy dared to beg for food. When no one was looking, Jeremy slipped him a piece of Mishmash-soaked bread.

"Well, Dwight," Mr. Ewing said, "it's the end of August. Tomorrow your punishment will be over. You

131

don't have to take care of the pigs all by yourself anymore.''

''All *right*!'' Dwight cried triumphantly.

''However,'' he continued, ''it's also time to check the *Wall Street Journal* and see if your commodities futures made any money.'' He reached behind him and grabbed today's paper from the bookshelf. ''I have it right here.''

''Don't bother,'' Dwight said with a resigned shrug. ''I checked the paper this morning. Pork bellies have been going down all month. I didn't make a thing.''

''That means Charlie and his friends lost money, too,'' Mrs. Ewing pointed out.

''I know, I know,'' Dwight muttered, resting his chin in his hands. ''Don't rub it in.''

''I'm not, honey,'' Mrs. Ewing said with a sympathetic smile. ''The commodities market is always a gamble. You took a chance and lost. I just hope you learned that investing isn't a way to make easy money.''

Luther chuckled. ''Guess you'll be lookin' for a part-time job this fall, Dwight. I hear Mr. Baum needs someone on Saturday mornings to help the customers carry bags of feed out to their trucks.''

Dwight groaned and went back to his food. The family ate in silence for a while, savoring the flavors of the Mishmash. When Luther was finished, he pushed his plate away and said, ''My, my, who would ever imagine leftovers could taste so delicious? And so easy to eat—even with my old false teeth.''

Mrs. Ewing chuckled. ''I always think of Mishmash Surprise as baby food for gourmet babies.''

Dwight leaned forward in his chair and said, ''You know, I read in the *Wall Street Journal* that baby food is big business these days. It's because all the yuppies

132

are having babies now and spending lots of money on them."

Jeremy licked the last of the Mishmash off his fingers. "Can we have this again tomorrow night?" he asked.

Mrs. Ewing shook her head. "We're out of leftovers. But I know some other mushy recipes. If your throat is still sore, we'll make one together."

"Well, well, well . . ." Mr. Ewing said suddenly.

The whole family stopped eating and turned to look at him. Mr. Ewing was staring into space with a dreamy, faraway look in his eyes. Slowly, his eyebrows lifted and three deep wrinkles formed across his forehead.

"What is it, Daddy?" Jody asked eagerly.

"Babies deserve a night out once in a while, too," he muttered in a husky voice. "And for parents who are too busy to cook . . ."

"Dad, what are you talking about?" Dwight asked impatiently.

"Imagine a restaurant that caters exclusively to babies," Mr. Ewing said dreamily. "Can't you just see it? We'd serve nothing but mushy food. Oh, everything would be jam-packed with vitamins and minerals and protein, of course. But the most important thing is that it would taste good to babies."

"I could decorate the place in a style that babies like," Mrs. Ewing mused. "Bright colors, baby-size furniture. And tough, unbreakable dishes."

"The idea has possibilities," Dwight broke in, "but it has to be promoted correctly. I'll handle the advertising campaign."

"I'll help Mom think up the recipes," Jody said.

"And I'll taste them," Jeremy announced with an impish smile.

133

"Wait a minute," Jody said, tossing down her bread. "What about the farm?" The idea of moving didn't seem as exciting as it once had. Yellow Bluff had begun to feel like home.

"Of course we'll keep the farm. But now that we've got seeing-eye pig training down to a science, we can train our next batch of pigs faster and easier," Mr. Ewing said. "That means more spare time—time enough to open a little restaurant out in the motor home." He glanced at Luther. "But it all depends on you."

"Me?" Luther exclaimed. "But I don't know the first thing about babies!"

"You don't have to. What we want you to do is take over as manager of the farm. We'll still help you train the pigs, of course, but you'll be in charge."

"Hmmm," Luther said, half to himself. "I could keep Curly for myself and sell Moe and Larry. Then after we bought the next batch of pigs, I could try out a few pig-trainin' ideas of my own." He laughed and slapped his thigh with the palm of his hand. "My son will probably blow a gasket when he finds out." Then he shrugged and said, "Well, you only live once. Might as well make it a party." He leaned back in his chair and grinned. "Folks, you got yourselves a deal."

"Hurray!" the Ewings shouted.

"We've got a lot of work ahead of us," Mrs. Ewing said. She looked pleased. "And a lot of decisions. We have to think up a name for the restaurant, plan the menu, design the decor . . ."

"I've got an idea," Jeremy said. "Let's name our new restaurant This Little Piggy."

"I can see it now," Dwight exclaimed. "We'll use a picture of Willy in the logo. And our advertising

134

slogan can be 'This little piggy cried, WEE, WEE, WEE, I WANT TO EAT AT THIS LITTLE PIGGY TONIGHT!' ''

The last word had barely left Dwight's lips when Willy jumped up into Jeremy's lap and let out an excited oink.

''What do you suppose he said?'' Mr. Ewing asked.

Jody pushed back her chair and jumped to her feet. ''He said, 'Skip the small talk. Bring on the Mishmash Pudding!' ''